BI

Steve Beed

ISBN: 9798393872168

DEDICATION

For Annie, who – amongst all the other things she does for me - reads my books and helps the writing be gooder.

CONTENTS

ACKNOWLEDGMENTS

'To live without love is not really to live.'

Moliere

"When you look for the bad, expecting it, you will get it."

Eleanor H. Porter

CHAPTER 1

IN THE BEGINNING

T he door swung open and Chris stepped inside, pushing it firmly shut behind him. For a moment he just stood in the hallway, listening, thinking, pausing. Then he took off his black tie, scrunching it into the pocket of his suit jacket before stepping into the kitchen and switching on the kettle. Everything in the confined space of the kitchen was in order, a place for everything and everything in its place. He selected one of his mugs from the mish mash of a collection in the cupboard (Homer Simpson, open mouthed, saying 'Doh!') and put a tea bag in, then stood and waited for the water to boil.

The room was tired, the stark light from the single fitting showed faded and worn tops from the last century, clinging to life as they showed the wear and tear of years of use. A small formica-topped table and two simple chairs dominated the middle of the room, also displaying the scars and badges of honour from their years of trusty service. On the table sat a neat pile of unopened mail. A window over the sink looked out over a compact garden, wilting after a busy summer of producing colour and life. It needed a tidy, stray leaves to rake, dead plants to remove, and maybe one last cut of the grass. It would have to wait for now though.

The kettle blew itself out and Chris filled his mug, then added some milk before fishing the tea bag out and taking the mug with him to the next room. Here he made for the small sofa, sinking into the well broken-in cushions with a sigh, putting his tea on the side table as he did so. He looked across at the empty armchair and then closed his eyes, tipping his head back against the roses that climbed the wallpaper.

The house was silent. There were no residual sounds lingering, no noise seeped in from outside. With his eyes closed he felt like he was floating, drifting in an empty black ocean. He stayed like this for some time, letting the silence have its way, then abruptly he opened his eyes. He reached for his tea, tested it with his lips, then drank it down in several large gulps before resetting it on the table.

Again, the stillness crept up on him. He got up, took his empty mug to the kitchen and switched on the radio on the window ledge. The sudden eruption of sound in the tiny room reached into the corners and filled the spaces. He rinsed out his mug while Radio 2 told him what the traffic was like in various cities around the country. Leaving the radio on, he climbed the narrow staircase to his room.

Unlike the downstairs rooms, this was freshly painted, bright and filled with the finest self-assembly furniture his limited budget would allow. A large desk dominated one wall, on it sat a computer that Chris powered up as he entered the room. He took off his suit, hanging it back in the wardrobe and replaced it with a pair of grey joggers and a faded, baggy blue sweatshirt with a Nike swoosh across the front. Comfortable now, he sighed, stood up and went back towards the sound of Rhianna in the kitchen. He took some bacon from the fridge and dropped it under the grill.

By the time the next song had finished the bacon had been turned over and a fresh mug of tea had been made. The smell filled the kitchen, making him impatiently bend to check the grill like a bobbing duck - he hadn't eaten since breakfast time. He busied himself buttering bread before lifting out the bacon, adding it to the bread and pulling out one of the two chairs at the kitchen table. The ketchup came reluctantly out of its bottle and covered the spaces between the rashers, oozing at the edges as Chris took his first bite. Once started it did not last long, washed down with generous swigs of hot tea. Chris clattered the plate into the sink with his cornflakes

7

bowl and carried his mug into the sitting room where he returned to his previous place on the sofa.

The sound from the radio was more muted now it had further to travel. It became the background to the sanctuary of the sitting room. Chris finished his tea and realised that, for the first time he could recall, he had nothing to do. He had plenty he could do, but nothing that he had to do. In the absence of the distraction offered by activity he sat thinking. In particular, thinking about the day that was now creeping inexorably towards its ending.

The funeral had been well-ordered. Everything clean, varnished, polished and perfect. The crematorium staff, in well-rehearsed fashion, making sure everything ran like clockwork. The preceding group of mourners had barely cleared the chapel before his group was ushered in. Afterwards, the following party were flocking crow-like at the doors even as Chris was shaking hands with the last mourner. He had known most of the attendees since he was a child, regular visitors to the house at one time or another – not so much recently – mostly called aunty this or uncle that, despite the fact they were not related to him.

It had taken Chris aback that nobody had appeared sad. He didn't know what he had expected; tears, wailing, gnashing of teeth and beating of breasts? Mostly, Chris thought, they had looked resigned, as if it was no surprise to them that their ranks were thinning. Chris had looked at their grey hair, wrinkled hands covered with liver spots and faces full of years. He understood then, as he stood watching the coffin slide silently along its runners and the curtains flap closed behind it, there would be a time when he would share this knowledge more fully, plenty of time yet though. Now, back at home, he was not so certain. He felt fragile and worn, as if the day had taken more than his physical energy and emotional strength – it felt as if it had taken part of his essence.

They had stood and talked at the edge of the gravel car park, Aunty Vi telling him how sorry she was, Uncle Bob talking about how lovely the service was. All well-rehearsed lines, but not platitudes - all sincerely meant. The sun shone in the incongruously blue sky, the birds calling to one another through the masks of greenery as they flitted to each new destination and back. Far away the sound of traffic ebbed and flowed, as people, unheeding of their proximity to the tragedy unfolding here, went about their business. Chris wanted it to be over, for the taxis to turn up and take everybody away, to be able to get into his car and just go home.

Now he was here, he couldn't recall precisely what it was that he had been so keen to come back and do. The house was still quiet even with the radio singing away in the background. Everywhere he looked were mementos and souvenirs of what had been. A shelf full of ceramic nick-knacks. A selection of crossword books, with a pair of glasses resting on top, on the side table. The faded brown corduroy chair with the crocheted multi-coloured blanket thrown over the back. Artefacts from 'before'.

As he stood staring blankly at the chair, he could picture her sitting there, remote control in hand, looking at him through her thick-lensed glasses.

"How was your day dear?"

"Yeah, okay. Just work, you know."

"Listen to you, you were just like that when you were at school."

She mimics his voice, "Okay, just school. What happened? Who was there? What did you do?"

Chris sighs;

"I really did sit in my office all day, there was a mix up with one of the orders, and it took most of the day to sort it out. You know what the suppliers are like when things aren't right."

This seemed to satisfy her, she shook her head sympathetically and made a tsk noise.

"There now, that wasn't so hard was it? Did you pick up some milk on the way home?"

"Yes, do you want some more tea?" He indicated the empty mug at her side.

9

"That'd be lovely," she handed him the mug, smiling, and he went into the kitchen. As he left, she unmuted the TV and it let loose a round of applause. He came back in to watch over her shoulder as he waited for the kettle to boil.

"Paris!" they proclaimed in unison, in answer to the questioner on the TV. They paused, waiting expectantly for the host to confirm the correctness of their answer, before Chris went back to finish making the tea.

"So how was your day?" he asked as he settled back into the sofa.

"Oh, busy, Jean came round this morning, she stayed here 'till gone lunchtime – you know what she's like once she gets going. Her Tom's moving away - for work."

"Where's he moving to?"

"Somewhere near London I think."

"She'll miss him then, he drives her everywhere doesn't he?"

"Pretty much, he drove her here. His car's lovely though, so big and comfy. She's going to have to start getting taxis."

"That'll cost a bomb, couldn't she get the bus."

"Jean won't get the bus."

"It's only 4 stops from here."

"Jean won't get the bus."

"Why not?"

"Well, it's the bus isn't it."

"Why can't she go on the bus?"

"Because Jean won't get the bus."

Chris stopped trying to make sense of this, he had ignored the unintentional slight towards his own car, a functional 10-year-old Ford. The conversation had taken place over the background noise of the TV. Now they both turned to it and simultaneously answered;

"Norman Wisdom."

Again, they paused as they awaited confirmation of their answer. It came amid a disappointed groan from the TV audience.

"Fancy not knowing that, surely everybody knows that." She tuts disappointedly at the TV then says;

"I met him you know."

Chris does know, she has told him this story many times before. There is, however, a pleasure in watching her face light up as she retells the story of how she met Norman Wisdom;

"They were making a film in the next town. My dad, your grandad John, took me over to see all the comings and goings, his brother had told him there was something going on the night before. We got the bus over, it was so exciting, we didn't expect to see anybody special, we were just having a nosey. So, we were standing at the side watching all the men running about getting everything ready, all big bits of wood with paintings on and huge cameras on legs. It was so busy, then he came out of a caravan, right in front of us. Norman Wisdom, as large as life he was, came right over to us and said hello, in that cheeky way of his. And then he asked if we were waiting for his autograph. Well, the only thing my dad had on him was the bus ticket, so he signed that for me. Lovely man."

There was a moments silence, she sat pensively, lost in that long-ago moment, then she added;

"He wasn't very funny."

Now Chris was surprised,

"Why do you keep watching all his films then?"

"No, not his films silly, him." She gives a small smile and half a laugh to herself at the expense of Chris's foolishness. "When we met him, he wasn't at all funny."

"Well, it must be hard to be funny all the time."

"I suppose."

11

The sound of the TV show took over again briefly, catching the lull in the conversation.

"What did you have for lunch?"

"Sardines on toast, we've nearly run out."

"I'll add it to the shopping list. Do we need anything else? I expect we're short of biscuits if Auntie Jean's been round."

"Cheeky! Actually though, we could do with some more digestives. What do you want for your tea?"

"It's all right, I'll do it. I was going to have some of those sausages with some spuds. That okay for you?"

"I'll just have one sausage love, I'm not that hungry."

"Ok" Chris agreed, knowing that she'd eat two if he cooked them. "I'll do it in a bit, I'm going to have a brush up first."

He finished his tea then stood up and blinked at the empty armchair, the radio was still talking to itself in the kitchen. He joined it, wiping his cheek with his sweatshirt cuff and filling the sink. He washed the few things that had accumulated and then abandoned them again on the draining board. Once he was finished, he stood with his hands on the counter looking out at the garden. Birds darted in and out of his view, exploring the feeders placed strategically around the bushes and trees.

With a sigh Chris made a mental note to at least go out and do some dead-heading this week. But not today. He went upstairs and looked into her bedroom, another job that needed doing he supposed, he had no use of her things now. Another job that was not for today. He picked up a framed photo from her sideboard, both of them on a beach smiling at an unseen photographer. He remembers the day, it was when he was 8 years-old. The arch of Durdle Door is clearly visible in the background of the picture, lit by a ray of dazzling sunshine. It was a whole week of glorious sunshine, they had stayed in a caravan and, in his memory, eaten nothing but ice-cream and chips all week and spent whole days on the beach and in the frigid sea.

He took the picture with him, closing the door up and putting the photo on the desk in his own room. The light was fading now and the glow of the screen lit up his face as he leant over it. He scanned his e-mails, mostly spam, and scrolled absently through his Facebook page, gazing at pictures of people's children, pets, dinners and evening walks. He saw nothing that merited a comment or response.

Closing the page he moved the mouse until the cursor was hovering over a new icon then paused. Did he want to do this today? Was it the right time? He almost left it, then clicked and opened the link to 'Mr Angree'. For weeks now he had been venting his frustrations online, allowing himself free rein in his opinions on all the things that had pissed him off. It had been surprisingly therapeutic to write down his anger, unleashing thoughts he would otherwise have kept to himself.

What had surprised him more had been the gradually increasing number of people that had not only chosen to read his diatribes, but had come back for more. It was only a small following, 257 to be precise, but it had been slowly growing. It was apparent that the things he found irritating also got on other people's nerves. Supermarket self-checkouts, celebrities with ridiculous opinions, people who drove as if they had never had a driving lesson in their lives, customers who didn't know what they wanted when they went into shops, shop assistants who didn't seem to know what things they actually sold.

His most recent post was simple, a list of people who he wouldn't piss on if they were on fire. He had been careful not to use the actual names of people he knew or might come into contact with. People already in the public sphere were fair game though. He had called it 'Shitlist', in a nod to the band L7. It had attracted a lot of responses, mostly people suggesting names to add to the list. He read through some of them;

'The guy down the road whose dog craps on the pavement.'

'My old English teacher who was obsessed with commas.'

'Anybody who sings along with songs on the radio in public.'

The list had grown substantially since he had last looked, with people catching on with the general theme and getting into the spirit of things. Some of the responses even managed to raise a small smile on his lips, in spite of the sombre day he was just finishing. He clicked off the site and started to settle down for the evening, making a mental list of the things he really needed to get done now that the funeral was over.

CHAPTER 2

THE MORNING AFTER

At 7.15 precisely the next morning Chris reached out from under his duvet and pressed the 'snooze' button for a second time. When the alarm called again, he tumbled out of bed in a flurry of mild panic. He stepped under the shower for the briefest possible time, fought with his recalcitrant trousers and rushed through his tea and toast. He tried to cut some corners and shave some time off his morning routine, but it was never going to be enough, it was a lost cause and he knew it. He arrived at work, slightly flustered, at exactly 8 minutes past 8.

He went directly to his office, each wall within touching distance and covered with shelves full of ring binders, in turn bulging with invoices, delivery notes and orders. The paper trail he needed to process and maintain to ensure a free flow of products. In truth, most of this information was duplicated on his computer. He squeezed around his desk and sat down, powering up the computer then waiting for it to go through the motions of starting up. Once it was satisfied that it was ready he did the two things he did at the start of every work day. Firstly, he checked that the overnight backup had done what it was supposed to do; it would be a pain to sort out if they lost all their information again, they found this out the hard way a few years ago. What a mess that was, it had been weeks before things finally got back to normal, although Chris did manage to persuade the boss that money spent on a new backup server would be a good investment.

Secondly, he opened his e-mails and checked the new arrivals in his inbox, looking to see what needed doing first, what could wait until later, what he could ignore for now and what he could delete without reading.

The backup had been fine, all tucked away safely on the server that sat on the floor in the corner of the room. The e-mails were more challenging, having had two full days to accumulate. He was in the process of starting to check these when a head appeared around the frame of the open door.

It was Beverly from reception, her face bore an expression of practised empathy;

"Morning Chris. Did everything go okay yesterday?"

"Morning Bev. I guess so, I don't have much to measure it against, thanks for asking."

"We were all thinking of you, I hoped he would let some of us come along, but he insisted we were needed here."

"Well, never mind, you sent flowers. They were beautiful, thank you."

Now Bev allowed herself a smile, a Bev special, more sympathy this time.

"If there's one thing we can manage its flowers, do you want a cuppa?"

It was true enough; a garden centre was a good place for that. Bev had moved to stand fully in the doorway by now. She was slightly younger than Chris, with a riot of unruly brown hair tied back loosely. She was wearing a standard green company polo shirt and fleece, covering what Chris guessed, from the available evidence, was a good figure. Not for the first time thoughts flashed through his mind about how he would whisk Bev off her feet and woo and win her, if only she would leave her husband. Not that he'd ever had more than polite office chat with her. He smiled back at her and answered;

"Yes please, that would be great."

"Be right back then."

With that she disappeared and Chris went back to sorting his mail, taking great delight in identifying and ditching all superfluous messages, click – delete – click – delete, gradually whittling down the number of messages. As he was in mid flow with this task he saw in his peripheral vision a figure come to his door. Expecting it to be Bev with his tea, he looked up and smiled. The smile froze, not quite fully formed, it was Lagrange. Standing there grinning with his moustache slightly higher on one side, as if half a smile was all he could manage.

"Morning, good to see you back at your station."

"Good morning to you too," replied Chris, trying and just about succeeding in keeping the contempt he felt out of his voice. Chris had been working here for nearly twenty years, sharing some good times with a team he enjoyed working with – lots of jokes and laughter, and a boss he got on with – Mr Potter (Jim), who treated everyone like they were part of his family. Two years ago last March Jim had come into work one morning, hung up his tweed jacket and then fallen to the floor, his grey hair turning pink where he cut his head on the desk on his way down. Naturally everyone went in to full blown panic mode, until they had established he was still breathing, called an ambulance and collected Mrs Potter to come and take over the panicking side of things.

It turned out to be not too serious, a lack of iron that necessitated large numbers of investigative procedures and resulted in Jim deciding to hang up his wellies and sell off the business as a going concern. It was bought up by GardenCo, a company that already had a large number of garden centres spread across the country, although locally everyone still referred to it as Potters. GardenCo had sent in a new, enthusiastic, besuited young manager called Gavin Lagrange, who was full of good ideas about how to improve everything. Mostly this had involved turning the inside area into a large gift shop/shopping area full of overpriced items with feel good slogans and sayings printed on them and things that people would never

17

imagine they needed until they saw it and decided it would make the perfect gift for a loved one. Scented candles, mugs, honey in jars with hand printed labels, children's books and other sundry nick-nacks.

He also brought with him all the companies that GardenCo had arranged deals and offers with, meaning Chris had to change the way he worked, saying goodbye to some small nurseries and growers who he had dealt with for years, and who relied on the garden centre for a large part of their income.

"Just saying, I know you've had a difficult time, but I did notice you were a bit late this morning."

"Yes, sorry, I overslept a bit. It was busy yesterday."

"Well, you know, I understand. I just try to keep everything running smoothly, you know me?"

Luckily Chris recognised this as a rhetorical question, because he certainly did know Lagrange – twat!

"Well, must get on."

"Yes, you must, see you later."

Lagrange went off to be busy somewhere else, Chris bent back to his e-mails. No sooner had he clicked off the screensaver than Bev reappeared holding two mugs of gently steaming tea. She put one on the desk, adjusted the other and clutched it in front of her with both hands, slowly shaking her head. She glanced back over her shoulder to check that Lagrange had gone;

"What an arsehole."

"You heard then?"

"Every word, I'm sorry. That's all you need right now."

"No need for you to apologise."

"I know, but you know…?"

Following this non-sequitur Bev smiled again and turned to leave,

"Best get back, before I get told off too."

"Sure, see you later. Oh, and thanks."

He picked the mug up and smiled, they both new he was thanking her for more than just the tea.

"You're welcome," answered the receding voice.

Chris settled back down to his catching up, quietly replying, authorising, recording, ordering and collating. Occasional trips to the printer, two steps across the room, to collect things to put on his 'file pile' broke the monotony. The final printer trip of the morning was to collect a sheet that he attached to a clipboard and took with him to the delivery area. Once there he checked off the inventory against the delivery notes with Tim. Once they had finished Tim invited him into his overcrowded shed and made him a cup of tea in one of the once-white mugs that he kept in his hidey hole.

"I'm leaving," announced Tim as they perched on a pair of rugged and grubby looking stools to drink their tea.

"Really? When?"

"Soon as possible, Lagrange is making me work out all my notice first. I've got a new job all lined up at B&Q, figured I might as well drive their forklift as ours. Better pay too, my mate says you don't have to hassle for the money if they ask you to go over hours, not like this lot here."

He nodded his head in the general direction of the offices. Chris looked at Tim, he had started working here straight from leaving school. Chris still remembered him as the diminutive, shock-haired, wide-eyed boy who had turned up on that first day. He had filled out in the intervening years, hair cut short and the start of a tattoo collection that seemed to be all the rage nowadays - not like when he was younger, his mum had assured him in an authoritative way, that did not allow for any differences of opinion, that 'tattoos were for sailors and prisoners', a conviction he still found hard to shake.

"Don't blame you really mate; I'll miss you though. I guess Lagrange will ask one of the youngsters to step up to cover you."

"I guess so, doubt he'll pay them any extra though."

"You're right there. How's Debbie anyway?"

"She's great, don't tell anybody, but she's getting fat,"

Tim winked at Chris and moved his hands around in front of his stomach, indicating the general shape of what a pregnant abdomen might look like.

"Fantastic mate, well done to both of you, congratulations. When's it due?"

"Not for ages, next year. Debs told me not to tell anyone, early days and all that, but I've got to tell someone. You know how it is?"

Chris did know, he knew exactly how good it felt to say something, let it out, make it real.

"You'll keep in touch, won't you?" He asked.

He put his hand on Chris's shoulder;

"Course mate, listen, seriously, you showed me the ropes when I first started, you saw me okay. I appreciated that, I don't know if I would have managed otherwise. I know I was a bit scared of you at first, but you're okay."

Chris shrugged the compliment off;

"You'd have done fine, you've got nous. You were a scrap of nothing though."

They both laugh.

"I'd have stayed if it wasn't for him," again, a nod in the vague direction of Lagrange's office. "We're going out for a drink on my last day, you should come and join us if you're feeling up to it."

Chris knew Tim well enough to know that this was his way of offering his condolences and sympathy, and appreciated it.

"I will, I'm looking forward to it already. Anyway, have a good afternoon, I'm back off to my cubby hole to make sure you've done these right." He picks up his clipboard and a bunch of delivery notes.

"Bev told me to make sure some weren't right, just to keep you on your toes."

"She told you wrong. Have a good one."

He walked back to his office, knowing full well that there were unlikely to be any errors. If there where he wouldn't bother Tim – he'd just sort them out, as he had done for years, not that he made many mistakes.

The afternoon passed uneventfully. Bev kept him supplied with tea and Lagrange kept him supplied with inane questions that he could have easily found the answers to himself - with a modicum of effort. He steadily worked his way through the backlog, although not so fast that Lagrange would wonder if he needed as many hours as he did. A number of non-essential items dropped to the bottom of the list that he would pick up over the following few days, but for today he was finished, he was able to shut down his computer and leave the building without encountering Lagrange again. He got in his car and was about to leave when someone knocked on his window, it was Bev. Chris wound down the glass;

"It's lovely to have you back, let me know if there's anything you need won't you?"

"Sure Bev, it's good to be back."

"Maybe come round for tea sometime?"

"Maybe, that would be nice," agreed Chris. Bev stepped back and Chris started the car and crunched it into gear. As he pulled away he wondered, not for the first time, why Bev was always so kind to him. Sure, they worked together and had known each other for a long time. But it was just work, and he knew from experience that didn't always mean the same as being friends, in fact they rarely did. Still puzzling over it he arrived home, switching on the radio and selecting a ready meal from his collection in the freezer that he put in the oven to start cooking.

Changed and refreshed, he checked his meal. Satisfied, he put it on a tray, along with a glass of squash and an apple. He carried them through to the lounge where he switched on the TV and settled down on his sofa to watch while he ate.

He looked over to the empty armchair.

"That looks lovely."

It didn't, it looked like what it was; a bowl of red sauce swimming with unidentifiable pieces of 'stuff'. It smelt too, again, nothing identifiable, just smell.

"It's delicious, are you sure you don't want me to do one for you? It won't take long."

"Oh no dear, you have yours, enjoy it. I'll just have a bit of something later. I'm not that hungry, and I've had an iffy tummy today."

Chris didn't really want to get into discussions about 'iffy tummies' while he was eating something that could have easily been identified as the product of the aforementioned 'iffy tummy' in question.

"Sure you're feeling okay? I can call the doctor if you want."

"Yes, I'm fine. It'll all be okay again tomorrow. Jean said she had a dodgy stomach last week, it's probably the same thing."

"Well, if you're sure. Let me know if I can get you anything won't you."

"A cup of tea would be lovely." She smiled and displayed the empty mug next to her.

"As soon as I'm done eating."

"Thanks love."

Chris finished eating and took his tray back to the kitchen. He set out two mugs and switched the kettle on, then checked himself and put one of the mugs back, looking through the door at the empty chair. He made himself a cup of tea and looked around the kitchen, he thought again about all the things he should and could be doing. He wanted to get rid of some of the antiquated kitchen implements whose only purpose seemed to be to hinder access to the things he actually needed. Some fresh paint, new curtains and replacing the cupboard doors would transform this room.

Soon, he decided, he would do it soon. With that decision made he took himself upstairs and switched on his computer. After waiting for it to wake up, he scrolled briefly through his email and his Facebook page. It was all the usual boring nonsense, he opened his blog.

One thousand, one hundred and three – or, in numbers 1103. This new number sat on his screen, and Chris sat and stared back in disbelief. Even as he watched, it increased by another 5 hits. It took Chris a few minutes to work out what had happened. Somebody had read his post and, amused by it in some way, had reposted it on their own much more popular site. This in turn had led to the huge increase in his own readership.

You wouldn't exactly say it had gone viral, but it had certainly had a boost. The comments section was steadily increasing too, as more people joined in on the joke. Names of individuals and generic groups and categories of people that should, in people's opinions, be added to the 'Shitlist.'

Chris scrolled through, reading them. Some made him laugh, others just seemed a bit obscure. None were mean-spirited or offensive as far as he could see. Although he had been serious when he wrote his original list, he was glad that it turned into something that was entertaining people and he guessed he had got the tone of it just right.

Spurred on, he opened a new blog page and typed into the title box – "What I should have said when my boss told me off for being late?" He then started to write;

"I overslept this morning, bastard alarm clock didn't do its job…" He followed this with a summary of what happened that morning, and a list of things he wished he had actually said to Lagrange. The abuse is colourful, creative and cruel. Although it doesn't cross into the realms of offensive, it is close in places. He signed off with a question; "What would you have said?" After a spellcheck and read through he pressed submit, then left it to do its thing while he went downstairs with his laundry basket and busied himself around the house.

A clean around the kitchen, put on the laundry, make a cup of tea, straighten the antimacassars, and empty the kitchen bin. Once it was all done he took his mug upstairs and nudged the PC back into life so he could check if his new post had picked up any hits yet. He was not sure if it would have the legs of the last one, certain that it was just a flash in the pan and interest would be waning now, returning to his previous select readership.

He was wrong. Shitlist now had nearly 1500 hits and the comments section was continuing to grow. The new post had already been looked at 257 times, like Shitlist, the comments section was growing steadily. Chris read some of the answers to his query about what to say to his boss. The general consensus so far seemed to be 'Fuck off!'

Other notable suggestions included;

'I know, I didn't want to come.'

'So what?'

'Duck! – his tough luck if he doesn't!'

'Yeah, I was with your missus.'

There were also some sympathetic comments from people who felt for his plight. One post was from a manager, saying how irritated he got when people who were being paid good money treated the place like a drop in centre. Many people had replied to him, all abusive, some quite aggressive. He was clearly swimming against the current here.

Chris studied the comments for a while, there was definitely a more edged tone to the comments for the new post. Still he did not think there was anything especially nasty, although some of the replies to the manager's response where a bit on the unpleasant side. He watched as the numbers of readers of each post gradually crept upwards, also, the number of people discovering some of his old blog posts was gradually increasing. Still not viral exactly, but it was hypnotic watching the numbers, to see them grow each time he refreshed the page.

Shaking his head and blinking, Chris realised how long he had been sitting in front of the computer. He refreshed the screen one last time – 1641 – then stood up decisively, went downstairs and put on his coat and left the house. He took the short walk through the cooling evening air to the Kings Arms. It was two roads along from his own house, past rows of the uniform red brick houses with walled off patches of ground in front. These areas were given over to people's bins, bikes, flowerpot gardens and some brave benches where people could sit in the sun and talked to neighbours. One or two gardens had filled with untended weeds and litter, but mostly they were well kept. The houses in this part of town were a throwback to the former industrial nature of the area – all the factories are long gone now. Many of the houses were still home to people he had known all his life, mixed with newly arrived families - in transit as they worked towards bigger and better houses in greener postcodes.

If you could look at these same houses 35 years ago you would see a bustling community, people talking outside their front doors, kids playing on the pavements, the occasional brave footballers or cricketers starting a game in the road before being shouted in for tea. Now everybody parked where they could on the busy street and hurried inside their houses, making sure the doors were locked behind them.

Inside the pub was a smorgasbord of darkly varnished wood, faded red velvet and a collection of optics and bottles that twinkled with the reflected light of the fruit machine. Roger was behind the bar as usual, leaning over with the paper spread out in front of him. He looked up as Chris came in;

"Evening Chris."

"Evening."

"Usual?"

"Yes please."

He started to pour a pint of lager, talking as he did so;

"Everything go okay yesterday?"

"Yeah, as good as these things go, you know?"

"I guess. Well it's good to get these things over, start to move on again. Many people come?"

"Just a few of her old friends. I didn't really expect many, just a small do."

"Fair enough."

By now there is a freshly sipped pint of beer on the bar and Roger is handing him his change.

"Think you'll stay in the house then?"

It hadn't actually occurred to Chris that he might move out, never even crossed his mind.

"Yeah, why wouldn't I? It's all bought and paid for."

"I suppose, some people just like to make a break, start over. I just wondered is all."

"Nah, I'm all right where I am. Anyway, you'd miss me if I went."

"Do you think so? It's so crowded I wouldn't even notice you weren't here."

They both smile as Roger indicates the sparsely populated bar with its chipped furniture and carpet patterned with a mixture of red flowers and beer stains. Chris took another sip from his beer and then carried it to a table where he sat down and placed it carefully on a beer mat. He thinks of this as 'his table' and he is as familiar with it as he is with the furniture in his own home. Although it is years since anybody has smoked in here, the table still bears the burnt scars of cigarettes that had missed the ashtrays that used to be the main decorative feature. The walls fade to yellow as they run up to the nicotine-stained ceiling that Roger seems in no hurry to revive. Chris settled back with a contented sigh.

The few other people in the room sat in isolated clusters. A young couple sitting quietly sharing their lovers' secrets. She was wearing what looked like her work clothes, smart, freshly returned from the office. He was in jeans and a leather jacket, they seemed comfortable together in spite of this sartorial mismatch.

Two other tables had sole occupants, both regulars like Chris. They had nodded in greeting as he entered, but in all the years he had known them neither he nor they had attempted to initiate anything other than the most perfunctory of polite conversations. Like him they preferred their own company, a chance to sit and quietly enjoy a drink and let the shreds of the day drop away before taking themselves home to prepare for the next round.

On the table furthest from Chris sat two young men, only recently old enough to buy their own drinks. Chris recognised them both, they lived nearby, had grown up in the area. Chris had seen them change from sweet babies in pushchairs to cheeky kids with perpetually grubby faces, to rude teenagers with bad attitudes. In the past they had tormented him sporadically, then they had dropped off his radar – or he off theirs. Now here they were again, adults drinking in his pub, glancing in his direction occasionally, laughing and talking to one another and swapping stories from their own days.

Chris didn't like them being there, he did not think of his pub as a skinny jeans/track suit/gold chain sort of a pub. Also, he was sure that they were laughing at him some of the time. Not that he was paranoid, but he knew that people did laugh at him, he knew well enough when somebody was trying to look at him surreptitiously, or talking about him when they thought he was out of earshot. A loud burst of laughter as one of the lads showed the other something on his phone shifted him from his thoughts, He did not think of his pub as a laughing out loud sort of pub either. He finished his drink and walked the empty glass over to the bar.

"Goodnight Roger."

27

"Goodnight, see you tomorrow."

"I'll be here, have a good one."

"You too."

With that Chris left the pub and retraced his steps through the darkening streets to home. He went straight upstairs and sat at the computer, curious to see how many more people had read his latest post in the short time he had been away. He was pleased to see that the number of hits and the number of comments had all increased. Satisfied, Chris started to work his way through his evening routine in preparation for settling down for the night; Old tee-shirt and pj's, brush teeth, put on cream, lay out tomorrows clothes and check the alarm clock is set. He double checked tonight, not wanting to piss of Lagrange again. Once done he settled down to tossing and turning until he was finally comfortable enough to doze off, half wrapped in duvet, half draped over the edge of the bed, but finally settled.

CHAPTER 3

IN THE NIGHT

Sometime later his eyes opened again, in the darkness. They did not open with a start or a jolt, just open-eyed and awake. Lying in the warmth of his bed he looked over to the clock without moving his head. Two o'clock, he sighed and closed his eyes again. Then he reopened them, something had not been right. He didn't know what, but it was off kilter. He lay still, eyes wide open now, and tried to work out what it was that was wrong. There was nothing out of place, nothing moving, no obvious thing that would have woken him, outside was silent. As he slowly moved his head and looked around the room his eyes adjusted and he looked deeper into the shadows and areas unlit by the thin slivers of moonlight that crept through the gaps at the edge of the curtains.

He decided it must have been the residue of a now forgotten dream or an outside noise long since passed. He closed his eyes again – the briefest split second before they were fully closed there was a spark of red from under the desk. Not the computer, no red LEDs on that, nothing that he could remember from the jumble of cables, plugs and sockets that inhabited the dark recesses. He opened his eyes and looked again, peering into the shadows, there was definitely nothing there now. He reclosed his eyes. Again, in the last possible moment before they were fully closed there was a spark of red. This time his eyes snapped back open and he peered into the space beneath the desk, lifting his head from the pillow and leaning forward for a better view. Nothing.

Fully awake now, Chris switched on his bedside light and leaned forward for a better look under the desk, just to check, but it still looks the same as it had before. He was about to switch the light off again, shaking his head and muttering to himself about what a prat he was being. At the precise moment his thumb hit the switch the shadows under the desk moved. He clicked it back on and slid out of the bed onto the floor and peered under the desk, in the far corner where he had thought he saw the movement. He bent down, putting his head under the desk to look again.

His head blocked out most of the light from his lamp, but as he looked, he saw the shadow move again. He stared as the dark recess started to fold in on itself, like smoke or like oil on water, fluxing and turning but never quite settling to anything – a lava lamp of shadows. He watched, mesmerised by the strange fluid motions. Tentatively he reached his hand forward, fingertips pushing towards the ephemera, they brushed the closest moving part of the black and felt nothing.

With no warning the red reappeared. Not a light though, a single blood red eye in the middle of the swirling shadow, attached to nothing, shining deep red and staring directly and unblinkingly at him. He jerked backwards, bumping the back of his head on the underside of the desktop and sat back on his haunches, leaning against the bed and staring right back at the eye. He put one hand on the back of his head as he sat unable to take his eyes away from what was happening beneath the desk.

Slowly a second disembodied red eye opened next to the first one. Around them the creases in the air seemed to take on a more solid appearance, spreading outwards. A snub nose, two outsized ears – pointed and upright like a cats ears, but not like a cat. A mouth in a rictus grin showing a range of discoloured and alarmingly sharp-looking teeth. The rest of the body appeared by increments, no more than two feet tall, jet black and sinewy, crouched down with its arms folded over its legs and an improbable pair of wings folded on its back. It continued to stare directly at Chris, unblinking, unmoving.

Unsure of how long he had been holding his breath, he exhaled loudly with an accompanying

"Fuck me!"

The grinning, razor toothed mouth stretched a little further and a cold voice replied;

"Maybe later." With an accompanying incongruous snigger.

"What the fuck…."

Chris finally regained some composure and started to lift himself back onto his bed, still not taking his eyes from the tiny monster in front of him. It started to unfold itself and move from its hiding place, keeping a steady distance between them as Chris withdrew.

"What the fuck?" Chris asked again.

"What the fuck?" mimicked the monster.

"What do you want? What are you?"

By now Chris was on the bed, he pulled his feet up off the floor and started to reach around for something to defend himself with. With no weapons coming conveniently to hand he settled on the pillow which he held in front of himself with both hands.

"I'm here to help."

"What?"

"Here to help."

"Help what? Why? What are you?"

"You do have a lot of questions." It was now out from under the desk and nimbly pulled itself up to perch on the edge, sitting facing Chris. Its black satin skin had an oily quality with an undercurrent of ripples and eddies. As it sat on the desk Chris could see it solid black mass most resembled the gargoyles found on the corners and edges of old cathedrals, spewing water from the roof and protecting the building from evil spirits.

The continued presence of the creature was disconcerting, nevertheless Chris found his heartbeat was slowly returning to something like normal and his curiosity was starting to kick in. After all surely this was just a dream, and so what if the creature was ugly, who was he to judge?

"What are you?" he repeated.

"Who. You mean 'who' am I?"

"Okay, who are you?"

"That's better. 'What' – how rude."

"And appearing in my room in the middle of the night isn't rude?"

"It's what I do." This was accompanied with a shrug, exaggerated by the wings on its shoulders, and a gravelly cackle of a laugh that outlasted whatever perceived humour there might have been in the comment. Chris waited for it subside then asked again;

"So, who are you?"

"Poquelin."

"What?"

"Poquelin. At your service." It made a nod of its head in an odd kind of bowing motion that threatened to topple it from its perch on the edge of the desk. The whole situation had changed from the alarm Chris felt at the appearance of the first eye, to the desire to giggle as the tiny creature with the French accent flapped its leathery wings to stop itself from falling. A glance from its fiery eyes and the slight curl of its lip, revealing an oversized incisor, convinced Chris that laughing out loud would maybe not be a good idea.

"How did you get here? What do you want?"

"I already told you, I'm here to help."

"Help what?"

"Just help, you know? A bit of this and a bit of that."

"What if I don't need your help?"

32

"Trust me, you need my help."

"What….but….how? I mean, what on earth are you talking about? What could you possibly help me with, and what are you anyway?"

"Not what – who? I am Poquelin, and I'm here to help you with some things you may have forgotten. It's so easy to overlook things, especially when you're so busy running around here and there, and you've had a lot on recently. I'm not the only one who's tried to help, lots of us have. We have been updating your list, it's incomplete. I know you've looked at some of the other suggestions, but the fact remains, your original list was incomplete."

"What list?"

"The one you made on this." Poquelin reached behind himself and clacked his elongated fingers against the computer screen.

Poquelin had somehow produced a tube of paper in one of his clawed hands. Chris did not see where it came from, it was just there. He held it up theatrically in front of himself and started to unroll it, looking over the top intermittently as he began to read out loud;

"Mrs Palmer, Mr Priestly…"

"Who?"

Poquelin sighed theatrically and read the names again.

"No, I mean who are they? Why are you reading their names to me? What is actually going on here?"

"See? This is exactly why you need me. You've got a memory like a sieve. Mrs Palmer put your picture in the bin – the old cow. You cried for nearly 20 minutes. She said it wasn't what you were supposed to be drawing – but it was the best picture of a space rocket in the whole fucking class.!"

"What? That was when I was 6! Why would I….do you know what, forget it, this is ridiculous."

"Mr Priestly made you clean the PE cupboard when you couldn't do PE, then gave you a detention for not doing it properly – the bastard!"

"Again, a lifetime ago. This is ….it's ridiculous."

"No, it's important to get these things right. If a job's worth doing and all that."

Poquelin let go of the bottom of the roll of paper and it dropped to the floor, he then started to read again;

"Toby Jones, poured his juice onto your dinner on purpose. Twat! Janet Cox. Sent you a letter asking you on a date then turned up with her friends and laughed at you. Hmm, maybe I should add their names too."

"For fucks sake!" Chris lay back on the bed, he put the pillow he was holding over his head and pulled the duvet up to his chin.

"This is the worst dream ever, just go away and let me sleep!"

"It's not a dream, and I've only just started."

Poquelin waved his scroll for emphasis and then continued to read, reeling off name after name of people who had at some stage in his life, committed some slight against Chris. He groaned and rolled over, shutting his eyes tightly with the pillow wedged over his ears. It wasn't enough to block out the scraping voice, he listened to the litany of crimes and miscreants being read out until, at some point, he fell asleep.

CHAPTER 4

STRANGE REACTION

"Good morning, it's lovely to see you again. I'm Bev."

Bev's smile came naturally enough as she greeted the young girl who had been taken on to work alongside her as receptionist/dogsbody. She was replacing Jill, who had left abruptly when Lagrange told her it was not okay to take time off for a hospital appointment. Bev didn't blame her either, she would be out the door like a shot if she didn't need the money. Although all the money she made yesterday had been negated by her idiot husband's decision to take the afternoon off and 'get in a round of golf'. His argument that it was good for his mental health had, needless to say, not gone down well.

Jill's replacement, Kiera – Bev remembered from their brief introduction two weeks ago – smiled back,

"You too, it's good to be here, but I'm sooo nervous."

"Don't be, you'll be fine. Most of what we do is just common sense, and nobody bites. I'll show you everything you need to know and just ask if you're not sure of anything."

"Thanks. I'm just so…I want to get it right. My mum's so pleased I've got a job here."

"I'm sure she is, come on I'll show you the most important things first, let's go and get a cuppa."

They made the short journey to the small staff kitchen area, the usual slightly grubby sink, stained mugs and tiny fridge that you would find in many workplaces. Bev started making the tea as Kiera reeled off a string of questions about what they needed to do first, did she need to set things up? Was she meant to have a name badge?

"One thing at a time, we'll get everything sorted out in good time, don't worry."

Bev heard Chris's distinctive footsteps approaching, on his way to his cubby-hole office.

"Grab another mug, Chris is here."

Obediently Kiera passed a third mug just as Chris passed.

"Morning Chris," breezed Bev.

"Morning," he stopped in the doorway and looked in.

"Just making tea now," she looked up from what she was doing. "God, you look like shit, are you okay?"

"Thanks for that, yeah I'm fine, just didn't sleep well."

"Well, if you're sure. Hey, this is Kiera, be nice to her it's her first day."

"Good morning Kiera, nice to meet you. Give me a shout if there's anything you need, mine's the door at the end of the corridor."

He took his mug from Bev, thanked her and continued to his office where he squeezed in and settled down to work."

"What does he do?" asked Kiera.

"Chris? He keeps this whole place going. If he wasn't here it would grind to a halt."

"Really?"

"Pretty much, he does all the ordering, pricing, rotas and paperwork, the wheels would come off if he wasn't here."

"He doesn't look like…"

Kiera's sentence trailed off unfinished. Bev looked at her, was about to frown. Then she remembered her own, similar, feelings when she had first met Chris. It was Kiera's first day, and she was only young;

"Do you know the saying 'don't judge a book by its cover'?"

"Yes."

"Well don't underestimate Chris, there's a lot more to him than meets the eye."

She had aimed to offer this advice in a kindly aunt kind of a way. Kiera did not appear chastised or upset so Bev guessed she had hit the right note. They took their tea back to the reception and Bev started showing her new colleague all the ropes and explaining what they did.

As the day wore on Chris gradually started to wake up, with sufficient caffeine to keep his brain engaged and a couple of spurious trips to see Tim and get some fresh air. Bev was busy easing the new girl into her role, so no chance to chat to her, instead he settled into his work. He made sure everything was in order, making some calls to ensure that the more popular autumn stock items were going to be ready in sufficient quantity from all the usual growers.

All the while he mulled over his weird dream from the night before. It had not felt like a dream at the time, but when he woke up in the cold light of day, he told himself it must have been – mainly because small monsters with wings and fangs don't really exist. But it had seemed real enough in the darkness of the night, he remembered his fear as it materialized and his disbelief when it started talking to him. The 'thing' had even had a name, although he couldn't remember it now, Velasquez – or something like that.

He was working on what he had decided would be his last job of the day, unless Lagrange came in with another ridiculous request for him, processing a bulk order from a local landscape gardener who he had worked closely with for a number of years. As he was transcribing the scrawled notes from his phone call onto an order form he heard a raised voice. At first he just ignored it and hunkered down to his work, determined to finish it off and be ready to leave on time for a change. He heard the voice again. This time he gave it more attention, it was Lagrange – probably on one of his regular rants. Chris could not hear the words clearly, but he definitely got the gist. Then he heard someone else, the second voice sounded scared, if you can hear that in a muffled distant voice, Chris was sure he could. He extricated himself from his office as quickly as his furniture would allow and started to walk towards the reception where the shouting had come from.

He came through the door to find Lagrange standing red-faced with his hands on his hips, watching Kiera as she rifled through a pile of papers. Her face was red too, her hands were unsteady and Bev was nowhere to be seen.

"What's up?"

"None of your business," snapped Lagrange, "get back to whatever it is your supposed to do that you're being paid for."

Kiera looked at Chris, a desperate pleading in her watery blue eyes. This time he addressed her directly;

"Are you okay Kiera? What are you looking for, can I help?"

"She's lost tomorrow's rota and needs to find it, you need to get back to work."

Chris looked again at Kiera, who had stopped searching and was now looking from one of the men to another and back again. Chris spoke to her again;

"It's okay, you didn't lose anything, Bev passed the rota to me to make some changes. It's in the tray by my office door."

Now he turned back to Lagrange. He took a brief pause then, with no rush of blood to his head, but complete composure and calmness, told Lagrange what he thought.

"It's done, nobody lost it, it's in my office. It's also in your in-tray if you could be bothered to look every so often. I send the rota to you every single day, in advance, for you to check, although the only thing you seem to make sure of is that you won't have to put yourself out and do some actual work covering for anybody."

He drew breath and Lagrange, looking flustered, started to open his mouth to speak. Before he could get a word out Chris continued;

"I have no idea why you think it's okay to make this girl cry on her first day, or even why you think it's okay to shout at anybody, what is wrong with you? You shouldn't talk to people like that. I will contact head office and tell them what you have done if you don't leave her alone."

For Kiera and the recently arrived Bev, who had returned during the middle of everything and had quickly figured out what was going on, this must have sounded as though Chris was threatening to report Lagrange for shouting at a team member. They were both quite surprised and impressed with the impact this had. Lagrange turned pale, opened and closed his mouth twice and then turned and stalked back to his own office without saying a word, slamming the door shut when he got there.

For Chris and Lagrange there was a different understanding. When Lagrange had first taken over as manager, he had bought some questionable practises with him from the last centre he had managed. Things that involved 'ex-display' and 'seconds' of high-end items like garden furniture selling for a fraction of their retail price – mostly to Lagrange's neighbours and friends. There were also deliveries of plants and flowers that were substandard and had to be dumped. While this was normal practise, it was not normal to 'dump' them at the manager's home address, after he had gone through and selected which were not up to par.

None of this would have come to light if Chris had been using the computer software the company provided, but the tech guys had agreed when they set up that it would be good to have tandem systems for a while – and Chris's system showed up things that the company one did not. When Chris questioned some of the transactions in a routine meeting with Lagrange there was an awkward, deathly, silence. At the end of this interminable pause

Lagrange did his best impression of friendliness and tried to persuade Chris that it was nothing. Chris did not take it any further, but he did keep copies of the backups from that time, and he did keep a close eye out for future discrepancies.

Now Chris turned back to Kiera and Bev. They were by the counter, Bev with her arm over Kiera's shoulders, she looked at Chris and silently mouthed 'thank you', as she returned to reassuring Kiera that everything was okay. He returned to his office to finish up for the day, wiping a fine film of sweat from his forehead with a slightly trembling hand as he manoeuvred back to his desk.

Bev made sure Kiera was okay, made her some tea, found some biscuits and reassured her that it wasn't usually like this. She kept glancing down to Chris's door, which remained open, as always. She could see part of his left arm and his shoulder as he leaned forward over the computer. Bev wondered, not for the first time, why he continued to work here, with Lagrange seeming to pick on him at every opportunity. Then, she kind of knew why really, and wished sometimes she was as brave as he seemed to be so she could speak out and speak up.

He waved and smiled as he was leaving, not stopping for a chat today. He walked up the corridor and through the door to the car park. She watched him go, wishing her husband would be as gallant – or at least not as much of a dick. If only he would stand up for something sometime, do something considerate or thoughtful instead of watching football, playing golf or drinking with his mates. Admittedly it gave her lots of free time, but it was kind of lonely sometimes too.

Chris arrived home still unsettled from the confrontation with Lagrange. What was he thinking of? Did he really just threaten the boss? He knew no good would come of it, but resolved to keep his head down as much as possible for the next few days - or weeks, or even months. It depended how long it took for Lagrange to find someone else to turn his attentions towards, Chris was confident he could weather the storm – he'd endured worse things than a bad-tempered manager of a garden centre.

He let himself straight out to the garden. The sun was still shining and the jobs he had promised himself he would get round to had not gone away. After a short wrestle with the tangled mower cable he cut the grass, releasing an invigorating layer of scent throughout the garden, seed heads and stray blades of grass floating through the warm sun-bleached air. He packed the mower away and got himself a glass of water, which he took some large gulps of before getting the secateurs. He worked his way around the beds, borders, baskets and pots, heads falling with a regular faint flop. He was soon on the second sweep, rounding up all the dead and dying flowers and petals he had missed the first time around. The hedge needed a trim and tidy, but most of the plants were in pretty good shape. He paused, finishing his glass of water, then stepped back into the kitchen.

"All done?"

"All done."

"You've done a good job, it looks a treat. The hedge could do with a trim though."

"I know, I can't do with faffing about with the steps and climbing all over it right now. I'll save it for a weekend job."

"Fair enough. Did any of the hospital plants make it?"

He looked at the selection of plants clustered under the window on a long thin bench. All of them had come from the centre, none of them had been given a chance of survival. Chris liked the challenge of bringing these sickly specimens home and trying to revive them. More often than not he failed, but occasionally he was able to pull one of them through and give it a new lease of life. At the end of the bench was a pot with what had been a dried collection of bare twigs, now there where tiny buds of green along the branches where leaves were waiting to unfurl. At the ends of the branches were the beginnings of what would open into a collection of rosebuds, given time and care. He picked it up.

"This rose might be on its way back, I think we may have saved it."

She squinted at it and then smiled,

41

"What colour do you think it will be?"

"I've no idea, it'll be a surprise. We'll have to wait and see when it opens, but it does look like it's going to be okay."

"That's good, you are clever. Why don't you put it over there next to the yellow flowers for now, you know I like to look out at the garden."

"I do yes, is that ok?" He put the pot between two others on the low wall by the edge of the grass.

"That's super, now I can keep an eye on it from here. I do like to see how it's all doing out there."

"Well now you can keep an eye on it for me. I can bring a chair out for you if you want to sit out here for a bit, I'll make you a cuppa."

"No, that's all right, it would be too much trouble."

"It wouldn't be any trouble at all, come on I'll get you sorted."

"No really, it's okay love. I'm going to sit back in the lounge, I'm still not feeling too clever. You can still bring me a cuppa though."

She smiled and made her way through to the other room and Chris washed his hands and put the kettle on.

He looked out at the rose, sitting in its pot on the wall. White, the blooms where white. A collection of small white buds crowded at the ends of the leaf covered branches. Chris smiled to himself;

"They were white," he said, to no one but himself and he wished that she had seen them. He started to peel some potatoes and put a pan on the hob ready to fry the piece of fish he had waiting in the fridge.

CHAPTER 5

MIDNIGHT CALLER

L ater that evening Chris checked into his Blog. He had resisted for as long as he was able, but finally gave in and looked at the numbers. To his surprise they were still increasing, more and more people had been adding comments and sharing it with their friends. Again he scrolled through some of the contributions. Again, some were funny, some were rude and some were risqué, although there were now a good smattering of messages that were just plain offensive. He read through some of them before clicking onto the tab that created a new post. He had been mulling it over for the last few hours, and even after his therapeutic gardening he was still quietly seething. He couldn't believe Lagrange had done that to the new member of staff – actually, he could, he had little time for Lagrange – or that he would provoke such a response from himself.

His fingers hovered over the keyboard for a moment, and then he began to type;

TWAT UPDATE!

This time he was succinct, describing what had happened and including his thoughts on what misfortunes he wished would befall Lagrange; shitting a hedgehog, finding the cheese grater during a power cut, gluing himself to his car. A range of ridiculous fates that he felt his newly found readership would be more than capable of adding to, hopefully providing some laughs on the way. God knows he needed them. He signed off and made the trip to The Crown for his usual evening pint to end the day.

He arrived at the pub just as the two young men from the day before were leaving, he stepped back to let them pass through the doorway unimpeded and they brushed past him as he held the door open, not even glancing in his direction as they consulted their phones and moved away briskly towards the shops. Chris shook his head to himself before going inside and being greeted by Roger;

"Evening Chris, usual?"

"Please."

There was a pause while Roger picked up a glass and held it under the tap.

"I see those lads where here again."

"Yeah, they just left, they've been coming in for a couple of weeks now. Nice to see some different faces for a change really."

"No offence taken," Chris smiled and Roger returned it with a small laugh as he passed the beer across the bar.

"You know what I mean though, maybe they'll bring in some mates and start putting some money in the till."

"Yeah, hope so." Chris groaned inwardly at the thought of his quiet local being taken over by crowds of youths in hoodies and football shirts. He looked around at the sparse scattering of people in the room and nodded a few hellos before taking his usual seat. Roger probably had a point; it didn't seem feasible that a business could keep going with such a small number of customers. Admittedly it got busier at weekends, but even so, you would be hard-pressed to describe it as bustling.

He finished his drink, taking leisurely sips as he mulled over the events of the day. On balance he felt it was more shit than not, although that probably had as much to do with being tired as anything else. He hadn't been able to shake off that stupid dream all day, the disgusting creature and its long list of half remembered names – most of which Chris had spent a lifetime trying to forget. He ran over the events of the afternoon in his mind again, had he needed to get involved? Yes, he thought he had, on balance,

Lagrange had been out of order. The new girl, so impossibly young, in the new work clothes her mum had undoubtedly helped her choose for the event, on her first day in a new job. Yes, he decided as he got up to leave, he needed to get involved or he wouldn't have been able to look his reflection in the eye.

"Night Rog."

"Yeah, have a good one."

Later, in bed, Chris looked over at his desk before he switched of his light, bending to check underneath it before he realised what he was doing and stopped himself.

"Ridiculous," he said aloud, switching off the light and adjusting the covers around himself.

"Ridiculous," rasped a gravelly voice from the dark under the desk.

Chris closed his eyes and groaned.

"Go away, you're a dream."

He hunkered further down into his pillow and pulled the duvet up around his shoulders, willing himself to be asleep. A pen hit the exposed back of his head, not the barrel, but the nib jabbing like a dart and making him yelp. He pushed the covers back and turned to face the desk. Two coal red eyes looked back at him in the darkness.

"Ridiculous," the voice repeated, this time in a high-pitched falsetto. Chris put the light on to reveal the oily-skinned creature, sitting at the back of the desk with its back against the wall and legs spread out in front, showing a pair of bulbous feet with long, clawed toes. It waved lazily to Chris.

"Hello again."

"Fuck off, you're not real."

With whip-like speed another pen flew towards Chris's head, this time glancing the side of his scalp as he tried to move out of the way. It still made enough of a contact to make Chris wince.

"Ouch! What are you? What do you want? And can you stop throwing pens at me?"

Poquelin sighed theatrically;

"We went through this yesterday – stupid. Firstly, not 'what?' but 'who?' – my name is Poquelin. Secondly, I'm here to help."

"Sod it," responded Chris, putting his head on the pillow and making an inarticulate groaning sound.

"I don't want or need your help, I'm fine, go away!"

"Fine? Don't need any help? I think we'll have to agree to disagree there – did you even listen to anything I said yesterday? Did you? All those people, and what are you doing about it eh? Nothing, that's what!"

"It is nothing, it's in the past, over and done. I barely even remember most of those people. Why can't you just leave me alone?"

Poquelin rocked forward, and with a flap of his scrappy wings to assist him came upright with surprising speed. He stood with his wings outstretched and pointed his stubby, clawed finger at Chris.

"Was it nothing this afternoon? Was it?" His voice began to rise as he spoke.

"Did you deal with that? Did you? Or did you just do what you always do and wimp out?"

Now Chris's voice started to raise too;

"I did not wimp out, I got him to stop what he was doing, and I made him back off."

"Yeah, but he'll do it again. You didn't finish the job, you didn't deliver the coup de grace."

"What? What else could I have done?"

"Think about it – you're the one who keeps saying you don't need any help."

Chris looked at Poquelin and shook his head slightly.

46

"I know I should be scared of you, but you're a bit of a twat you know."

"Ooh! Now who's getting all macho? A bit late really though, you needed to channel some of that inner warrior this afternoon."

"I don't know what you're talking about, and I don't care – piss off and let me sleep."

With the same flexing of wings and astonishing speed as previously Poquelin sprang onto the bed, landing with one foot on the pillow and his ugly yellowed fangs, snub nose and crimson eyes pushed up against Chris's face.

"You should have punched his fucking face in."

"Eh?"

"Punched his stupid face, smashed his teeth in, nutted him."

"Why the fuck would I have done that?"

"To put him in his place, he's a bastard. He'd do it to you if he got half a chance. You need to get in first."

"Are you mad? Violence never solves anything."

"Seriously? You really think that? Are you naïve, or just thick as pig shit? I've never heard anything so stupid in my life, 'violence never solves anything.' I've seen men reclaim their wealth in a sea of blood, women like banshees - avenging stolen families, whole nations take back what belonged to them from crumbling ruins of dust blown cities. Violence has been solving things for hundreds – no, thousands of years. 'Violence never solves anything.' Bollocks."

During this Poquelin had stood arms and wings waving and gesticulating. Now he stopped and sat legs crossed on the pillow, leaning against the headboard with a satisfied smirk. Chris sat up and looked at him incredulously;

"Seriously – how did it make any of those things better? Did it bring back dead babies or mend broken men? Did it fix anything?"

"I'm pretty sure it made some people feel better somewhere along the line, it bought justice and closure to people who'd been wronged, it returned lost and stolen belongings."

"There's always a better way."

"Weeell, actually, sometimes there's not. You should have belted him."

"But I didn't and the problem was solved."

"Was it though? Was it really, or is there still time for things to come undone? Will he just wait, bide his time before he tries to get his revenge? You're going to need to watch your back now, you never know when or where he's going to get you back."

Chris sighed, he knew Poquelin was right about this at least, but he didn't know what he could do about it. Also, if he was being honest with himself Poquelin had made quite a compelling case for the use of violence and a part of him wished that he had done what Poquelin suggested and smashed Lagrange's face in. Not that he was equipped to give a beating to anyone, short overweight and unfit. He'd never been in a fight, but if he had he was pretty sure he would have come second, regardless of who it had been with.

Poquelin was on a roll now, in a manner similar to the previous evening he began to list things that Chris could have done to Lagrange; ludicrous, violent, obscene and at times ridiculous;

"Bash his brains in. Knee him in the balls. Jab your finger in his eye. Strangle him – with a football sock. Push him in front of a lorry and watch his body get smashed then dragged along the road."

As before, the list seemed endless;

"Douse him with petrol and burn him alive."

Chris switched off the light and rolled over.

"Poison him and watch him writhe in agony."

He pulled the pillow around his ears in an attempt to block out the litany of creative ways to maim, mutilate or kill Lagrange.

"Hang him and watch him wriggle, gasping for breath."

Eventually sleep took hold of him while the excited croaking of Poquelin's voice rang in his ears.

"Tie him to an alligators' tail."

CHAPTER 6

YESTERDAY AND TODAY AND TOMORROW

Bev arrived home and put her coat and keys in their place by the front door. There were no calls of greeting as she arrived, just a sullen silence that permeated the house. Of course, Dave would have finished work an hour ago by now, he would have chosen to go to the club for a 'cheeky half' before coming home Perish the thought that he should come back first and start getting the tea ready or anything useful like that.

Polly would also have found things to do, people to see and places to go after finishing university for the day – Dave had persuaded her to study locally to save money - most likely she would be going to her boyfriend Fred's house, from where she would text sometime in the next hour or so to say she was eating there and would see them later.

Anna was her given name, but her sunny disposition as a toddler had led to Bev calling her Pollyanna – subsequently shortened to Polly and then kept. Nowadays, when she was at home, that childish enthusiasm was in short supply, she was a ghost-like presence in the house, staying in her room much of the time, only venturing out for food, perfunctory conversations or passing through on her way to somewhere she would rather be.

Bev made herself a cup of tea in her favourite mug, the one with a scrollwork of flowers and leaves that held a generous volume of liquid. She sat in the quiet kitchen and wondered how a house that had once seemed so full – full of noise, laughter, people, could now feel so empty. Not that it was always like this, but it seemed to be more and more often these days. Between her and Dave they had spent years working long hours and living mostly frugal lifestyles, he had been keen to repay the balance of their mortgage as early as possible so they could live debt-free in their later years, maybe even retire early. He had monitored the balance obsessively, seeking out the best mortgage deals and constantly looking for ways to save some money and pay off a bit more. She wished he had spent less time working and a bit more laughing, taken Polly and her on some nice holidays, enjoyed some time together while Polly had still wanted to spend time with them. Wishing for things that had already gone was pointless, she knew that, but with the house nearly paid for she wanted to try and claim back some of that lost time. She didn't know how to start and was afraid it was already too late.

Her mind wandered to the incident from the afternoon. She had only been away for a few minutes, a quick comfort break, and had been sure Kiera could manage whatever came her way while she was gone. Clearly, she was wrong, it took her some time to work out what was going on when she got back. Kiera was upset and she had gone to comfort her and find out what had happened. At the same time, she had been listening to the heated exchange taking place a short distance away. Lagrange was the more agitated of the two, red-faced, flustered and angry. Chris had been calm and kept his cool. What was it he had said? 'I'll tell head office what you did' -what did he mean by that? What had Lagrange done that meant Chris had enough hold on him to make him back off so quickly and completely? Whatever it was, she was glad it had got rid of him and given her a chance to get Kiera calm and everything back on track, what a thing to happen on the girls first day.

Finishing her tea, she started cooking. Nothing fancy, nothing that would spoil if Dave was late back again, enough to share with three if Polly did decide to come back. Once it was all in progress, she got herself a drink, time for wine now the cooking was on - and she waited.

CHAPTER 7

I TOLD MY MUM

Some days are easier to arrive in than others. For Chris this day was one of the less easy ones. He felt tired from his second night of bad sleep, and apprehensive. This nervousness started when he woke and looked around the room for Poquelin, who was thankfully absent. It stayed with him as he ate his cereal and made his sandwich for lunchtime, he tried to imagine what retribution Lagrange would be planning – then tried not to imagine it, not wanting to know what fate would befall him. The trepidation followed him around the house, it came in the car with him and dragged itself across the car park into the building, joining him in his office where it sat with him waiting for something to happen – waiting for its time.

Bev bought him a morning mug of tea, she didn't stop for much more than a perfunctory chat;

"Morning, how's things?"

"All fine thanks, and you?"

"I'm good, I need to get to the desk, make sure Kiera's okay and keep Lagrange away from her. See you later."

She hurried off to make sure her charge had not attracted any more unwelcome situations. She needn't have worried, Lagrange was nowhere to be seen, there was no sign of his presence other than his car in the car park, he did not emerge from his office.

Similarly, Chris did not leave the sanctuary of his office, remaining firmly ensconced with his computers and folders and his sense of impending doom.

Bev appeared with more tea during a morning lull.

"Thought you might need another by now."

"You thought right, thanks."

"All quiet here?"

"All quiet, how about your side? How's Kiera?"

"Okay, she seems a bit quiet, not surprising really. Have you seen him today?"

"No, he's keeping his head down isn't he? I'd think maybe he's embarrassed, but it's more likely he's trying to figure out how to save face."

"Well, that ship's sailed hasn't it? Anyway, how are you getting on – at home and everything?"

"Oh, it's fine, a bit quiet. I've still got loads of stuff to sort out."

"Tell me if you want a hand, honestly I won't mind."

"Nah, it's kind of a one-person job really. I just need to get myself motivated for it, you know how it is?"

Bev didn't, but nodded anyway.

"How are all yours anyway? Polly doing okay? How are her studies going?"

"Ok as far as I can tell, she spends more time at her boyfriends than at home. I feel like we're a laundry service come cash machine at the moment. I guess that's the way it goes."

"I guess it is, we were the same when we were her age I'm sure."

Even as he said this Chris knew it was not true, when he was Polly's age he barely left the house and didn't have anyone he could call a friend – let alone a girlfriend – that he could stay over with.

But he was sure he would've if he had had the chance. Bev looked thoughtful, maybe even wistful, for a fleeting moment, then replied;

"I know you're right, still, it's hard when they don't need you anymore. Especially with Dave out of the house so much."

Chris didn't really know what to say next, he paused then took a good-sized gulp of tea.

"Anyway, thanks for this. I'd best get on, look busy just in case his highness does decide to show his face."

"I suppose. I'll see you later, and seriously, if you need a hand let me know."

"Will do, thanks. I appreciated the offer."

When days go wrong they go spectacularly wrong. For Chris the day had started ominously, but had managed to rehabilitate itself to tolerable by midday. At this rate there was every chance that it could end up being an okay day by the time he went to bed. If he could get to sleep without another of those ridiculous dreams with Velasquez, or whatever its name was, it might even stretch as far as being a quite good day.

With this thought in mind, he left his office to collect his sandwich from the staff kitchen. Lagrange had only left his office once, to run some unnamed errand, returning shortly after he left without apparently speaking to anybody or making any eye contact. With the coast clear Bev had despatched Kiera to the kitchen at the same time as Chris was there. He had just sat down and taken a bite of his sandwich when she came in, she appeared hesitant and hovered in the doorway uncertainly.

"It's okay, come on in and take a seat."

Chris indicated the other chair at the small round table and took another bite of his sandwich.

"I'm perfectly capable of standing up for myself you know."

"Huh?" Chris swallowed and looked up again, taken aback by this unexpected announcement.

"Yesterday, I didn't need your help. I was dealing with it."

"Okay." Chris was bemused by this turn of events, his recollection was that Kiera had been crying and scared, but he realised that she was probably embarrassed about this now, trying to save some face.

"I'm sorry," he said, "I hadn't meant any offence, I was just trying to help. Mr Lagrange can get a bit scary sometimes, if you don't know him."

"And don't patronise me, I'm not a kid you know."

Now Chris really was confused. He had thought he was doing the right thing yesterday, now he had serious doubts, had he really needed to get involved? This had all turned upside down too quickly for him.

"Ok, sorry. Really no offence intended. Have a good afternoon ok."

He started to pack away his half-eaten lunch with the intention of getting back to his safe space and getting back on with his work. Kiera though was apparently not finished;

"I told my mum, and she told me to keep clear of you."

"What?"

"She told me what a creep you were and to stay away from you. She said you were always like that and I shouldn't let you pester me."

Kiera's eyes had looked into every corner of the room while she was talking, dancing all around Chris without ever settling down to make eye contact. They finished by staring at the floor, looking at their respective feet. Chris felt himself flush, he opened and closed his mouth before asking;

"Why would she say that?"

"She knew you at school. She said you used to bother the girls then too."

Chris stood silent, Bev had arrived and was standing in the doorway behind Kiera. Her face had a look of disbelief – mouth open, hand to cheek, eyebrows raised. Kiera carried on;

"She said if you didn't leave me alone I was to complain about you, and tell you to leave me alone 'Quasimodo'."

Still Chris could not find any meaningful words, he looked at her face and realised he could see enough in her features to recognise who her mum was, the person who had coined the nickname Quasimodo when they were at school – and persuaded others to do the same. The same person who had systematically made his life such a misery that he had ended up not going to school at all. Janet Cox. He said the name out loud, then left his half-eaten lunch on the table and edged around Bev and out of the door.

"I'm not feeling well, I'm taking the afternoon off. Can you tell Lagrange when you see him?"

Bev watched him go, she considered following Chris and talking to him. She had heard enough of what had been said to understand what had happened. He really did not look like he wanted to talk right now, instead she stepped inside the kitchen, kicked the door wedge away and closed the door. Kiera looked simultaneously petulant and guilty.

"He is one of the nicest, kindest men you will ever be lucky enough to meet. He risked his job for you yesterday. Why on earth would you say those things to him?"

Her tone was questioning, she thought she had managed well to keep the anger and hurt she felt out of her voice. Kiera looked up defiantly;

"I don't like him, my mum told me what he was like."

"What did she tell you? I bet she hasn't even spoken to him for years. I bet she hardly knows him at all."

"She does, she went to school with him. She said…"

"I don't care what she said." No attempt at keeping the irritation out of her voice now, it was all she could do not to shout.

"He's never done anything to hurt anybody, he'll go out of his way to help people. He's such a nice man."

"Yes, but, look at…"

"Look at what?"

"Well, look at him."

"I do look at him, I see someone who has had to put up with this all his life," her voice was softer now.

"Honestly, I've known Chris for years, he wouldn't do anything to hurt anybody. I really think you need to get to know him, and maybe think about how you made him feel."

Bev left, closing the door behind her. Kiera, left alone, looked down at Chris's sandwich, confused and conflicted and holding a lunch that she would never eat.

CHAPTER 8
NOT AGAIN

Now that every possibility of this being a good day had been obliterated Chris sat in his car outside his house, hands clenched on the steering wheel. 'Quasimodo' – he couldn't remember the last time he had been called that, but he could remember how it made him feel. He felt the same now, the mixture of self-loathing and anger were a toxic blend, blotting out all other thoughts. Janet Cox's fourteen-year-old face occupied his mind, her laughing sneer, her hurtful comments and the shouts of 'Bonnie Quasimodo' every time she was in the same room, corridor or street as him and his back was turned. The way those taunts and the ensuing humiliation had increased after she had been caught bullying him by a member of staff and given a week's worth of detentions.

He had really thought he was over it, that time had provided some protection and he had moved on. But now Janet Cox had come back to torment him in the form of her daughter. He felt sick and hurried into the house, blurred vision making it hard to mate the key with the lock, and went to the kitchen for a glass of water.

"You look flustered, what's up?"

"Nothing, I was just rushing that's all."

"Are you sure? I don't want you getting ill too, who'd look after me?"

"I'm not ill, I just got stuck in the roadworks by the park. It's mad, all the lights are out of sync, the police had to come and sort it out in

the end. I swear there's not a single road the council haven't dug up this year."

"Well, you didn't need to rush."

"I didn't want you to be on your own for too long, how are you feeling?"

"Oh, about the same, I'm sure I'll start to pick up soon. Tomorrow's a new day."

"Well, you look dreadful. How's Aunty Jean?"

"Thanks, she's fine. She came on the bus, said it was so straightforward she doesn't know why she didn't do it before, instead of always having to waitround for her Tom. I might use it to go into town when I'm up and about again."

Chris looked at her. He didn't think she would be going on the bus any time in the near future, her eyes were sunken and her skin had no colour to it, drawn tightly across the bones in her face lifting her cheeks and making her smile thin and stretched. She took the glass of water delicately and sipped carefully from it.

"Ooh, thanks, that's better. I was parched. Are you going to watch TV with me in a bit?"

"Yeah, I'm going to make some tea first, do you want some?"

"What are you cooking?"

"Pasta."

"I'm not that hungry, I'll just have a bit if that's okay."

"That's fine, I'll dish you up a kiddie's portion."

He knew she would only pick at it, but it was better than nothing. She was starting to look thin and would need to start eating something if she was going to get better.

He took a sip of his water and leaned against the counter. Janet Bloody Cox, how he wished he had never heard that name again. Except he had – two nights ago, and now again today. He knew that

59

people he'd been to school with still lived in the area of course, just as he did. Mostly when people recognised him, which they invariably did, they averted their eyes, ignored him and pretended not to see him. Occasionally there where grunted or inarticulate greetings while passing quickly by. This invisibility suited him.

CHAPTER 9

THAT WAS THEN

When Chris was born his spine and pelvis where not lined up properly and one of his legs had a length advantage on the other, which it would maintain all his life. Being twisted and broken had not impacted much on his early life, consisting mostly as it did of rolling on the floor. But as he grew and the need for mobility became an issue, the tortuous process of stretching, wrenching and cajoling his bones into an appropriate skeletal format began.

There were, of course, operations. Numerous sessions on the table that pinned, cast, reset, bound and tethered the offending joints and supports. These were accompanied by specially constructed frames to keep him upright, looking more like medieval torture devices than cutting edge medical equipment. Along with hours of painful therapy, they achieved their aim. In spite of his tears and nights spent sleepless through the pain, they did what they were supposed to do. Chris was enabled to maintain an upright position, that meant he could take unstable and tentative steps with leg braces and a supersize shoe that completed the ensemble. They made him as well-balanced as he could be, which wasn't very.

The process was long, painful and arduous, although he rarely cried or complained once he was on the road to mobility. He pursued his goal of independence diligently and doggedly. By the time he was old enough to start school he was able to propel himself confidently about the place with the aid of two crutches for balance. This was not, in the opinion of the headmistress, a safe form of manoeuvre and his school career was delayed for a year while he perfected the slower and far more precarious art of moving without the aid of his crutches.

With this skill mastered he was re-presented to the headmistress, who reluctantly agreed to admit him with the caveat, 'on your own head be it!' Although he was not as steady or safe as he had been, he was able to move freely around the school, in his own time. His time was not as rapid as the other six-year-olds, nor as graceful or lithe. He was frequently left behind, and could regularly be found trying to get back up, having overestimated his own ability and overbalanced. In spite of this he was happy to be at school at last. When he couldn't join in other children's games, he shrugged it off and found quieter things to do, usually alone. When they nudged or tripped him so he fell to the floor – to much hilarity – he brushed himself off, he was used to the bruises and bumps of regular falls after all. And when they called him 'spaz' or 'crip' he did not take offence, because he didn't know he was supposed to.

As time went by his balance improved and he found he was able to coordinate his movements more efficiently, giving him extra speed. Still not as fast as the others yet, but working on it. He also started to form some tentative friendships and enjoy the semi-celebrity status that being the class cripple gave him. The teachers goaded him on; 'get a move on boy, keep up. If we make exceptions for you, we'd have to make exceptions for everybody – then where would we be eh?' Chris didn't know where they would be, but he tried to do everything at a speed that might avoid him being singled out, ridiculed or berated. The friends he made continued to refer to him proudly as 'my friend spastic Chris', which he preferred to the teachers nickname of 'hop along'.

Much later Chris would come to recognise these names for the hateful insults they actually were and see that they came from a place of ignorance and fear. But for now, they were terms of endearment, affectations rarely gifted to other children in the class unless they did something wrong. But that was different right? This was a good time for Chris, sitting at the side with the sick kids watching PE lessons, being spared the slipper for his indiscretions because the teacher couldn't quite bring herself to 'hit a cripple'. Spending time at the side of the playground with other children too scared or slight to join in with the raucous games of football, British Bulldog or monkey one two three and in, that he was too unsteady to share. He had tried, but it invariably ended with him being prostrate and bloody.

It was his need for speed that was his undoing. Constantly trying to move faster, he took more risks and felt more alive. Sure, he occasionally misjudged things and took a tumble. He would get up and brush himself off then be more cautious for an hour or two, until he fell again. Sometimes he would be slower to rise, with a tear in his eye and a new bruise, or a cut or gouge that needed tending. His mother was always there, applying a loving hand and another plaster and lovingly but proudly telling him to; 'slow down Chris, you'll get there the same however slow or fast you go.'

One January afternoon, having successfully navigated his way home along the icy pavements, refusing to hold any hands such was his fierce desire for independence. He had limped, swivelled and lurched his way back to the house, where he sat in the kitchen growing a snow-white milk moustache and eating his daily ration of two pink wafer biscuits, while his mum banked up the fire to warm the house and get their blood flowing again.

All of these memories lived in Chris's mind on a daily basis, fermenting and circulating. They formed the background to his waking thoughts and actions, as they do for everyone, an unspoken entity that occasionally surfaces at surprising and seemingly random moments. These experiences and micro-moments form our worldview and shape the way we behave and the choices we make. What happened next was something that Chris would love to forget, to obliterate from his mind and not have to relive in the dead of night when he couldn't sleep, or when he stopped to think about anything too deeply or for too long.

Finishing his milk, Chris got down from the table and went to join his mum in the sitting room where he planned to share the warmth of the fire and maybe persuade her to sit with him for a while and share his favourite story book; 'Where The Wild Things Are' by Maurice Sendak. He moved with his usual urgency and attempt at speed. He moved with his usual clumsiness and instability. He misjudged the space and distance entirely and bounced into the side of the armchair, which in turn bounced him into the fireplace. The fireguard was still to one side and his head landed in the newly heaped and freshly burning coals, catching his hair on fire, melting into his cheek and eye socket and filling his nostrils with the smell of overcooked meat.

Screaming, both him and Mum, she pulled him from the fire place and tried to steer him to the kitchen where she could put some cold water on his face. Her shouts for help went unanswered as she began pouring jug after jug of cold water onto his head and face, careless about where it splashed and pooled on her usually pristine kitchen floor, trying to cool the flecks of still smouldering coal that had embedded in his cheek. After the initial shock the hurt started to kick in and Chris's screams intensified as he started to feel the crispy flesh around the right side of his face and eye start to pucker and crease as the heat from the flames finished its work.

The ambulance ride (where did that come from?) and his arrival in hospital became a blur of events that he could rarely make sense of in his memories; Who? What? When? Where? He couldn't say, although he was eventually sedated so the doctors could start to untangle what had happened to him and decide what they should do about it. He slept, and when he woke, bandaged and screaming, someone came and helped him to sleep again. Eventually he found he could bear the pain enough to stay awake for periods of time and feel his damaged flesh under the bandages being rejected by his body.

He did not go back to school that year, nor for most of the year after. Instead, he went to hospital. Treatment after treatment after surgery after surgery. It was a long time before anybody offered him a mirror, he had guessed from the looks on people's faces it was not good. The averted eyes and looks of shock and involuntary disgust did not escape him in spite of his young age, he wanted to know. When he saw himself, he studied the crevices, scars and dead flesh with interested disgust, sharing the horror that others had shown. The blackened and puckered flesh around his eye and cheek, the reduced ear and pink bald scalp on one side of his head were not a good look.

After all the appointments, plastic surgery and skin grafts the surgeons thought his young body could tolerate, he was given a clean bill of health. By some miracle he had retained the sight in his eye, it stared out of a socket with no lashes or eyebrow, and permanently wept a trickle of salty tears down the side of his face where it drooped slightly. His skin was pink and smooth with unnatural ridges and bumps where it had been joined together, they had done all they could to salvage as much as possible of his original face, although there was no escaping the fact that half his hair and half his left ear were missing.

That Easter, when the doctors said Chris was ready to restart school, his mum took him back to make the arrangements. The same headmistress as before sat in her military smart office, devoid of any evidence that there where children anywhere in the building, and looked away from Chris. Speaking to his mother as if he wasn't there she said;

"I think it might be unsettling for the other children."

"I'm sure they'll get used it quite quickly."

"Well couldn't he wear a mask or something like that?"

"A mask? What kind of mask?"

"Oh, I don't know, I was just thinking aloud. I would worry that he wouldn't be safe that's all."

"Safe from what?"

"Oh, I'm sure you understand, I wouldn't be doing my job if I wasn't thinking about the others. Is he all there?"

Chris wanted to speak, but had been ordered by his mum to 'sit nicely and stay quiet', so that was what he did. His mum had been quite hard to predict recently - since his dad declared that he couldn't put up with all these appointments anymore. He had promptly disappeared to Manchester with another, younger, woman that Chris had never met. He had heard her talked about in guarded but disparaging terms when mum was holding court with her friends in the sitting room and he had been left to play in the kitchen with his toy cars, with strict instructions not to bother them unless it was an emergency.

Those friends now looked at his mum with even more sympathy than they had previously, when they would tell her how they were sure that Chris's scars would hardly show eventually (they were wrong) and that he was still a handsome clever boy (they were partially right.)

In truth Chris didn't miss his dad that much, he had spent most of his time between work and the pub, only appearing at home for sleeping, eating and a change of clothes. At weekends he went to watch the football, he never offered to take Chris. Chris thought his own inability to kick a ball without falling over had been a disappointment to his dad. In his own mind this translated into him being a disappointment, it would be many years before he realised that the fault was not his but his dad's.

"Yes, except his ear. Why would having some scars make him daft?"

"Well, I have to check. I wouldn't be doing my job if I didn't."

"He's the same boy that was here before, he had an accident that's all."

"I understand."

Chris wondered if she did, she didn't seem to. He sat quietly, as instructed and distracted himself by practising his newly learned 7 and 8 times tables silently in his head. The headmistress ignored him completely (apart from the occasional sideways glance) and told his mum;

"I think it would make more sense if we waited and he joined back at the beginning of the next school year, don't you? It will be better for everyone. Did you consider St Boniface?"

Chris had been paying partial attention, now he stopped counting and tuned back into the conversation between the two women. He knew what St Boniface was all right, it was the home where the simple kids went to live, the ones in wheelchairs who couldn't talk or go out and about like normal people. Bonnies the other kids called them, being referred to as a 'Bonnie' was about as big an insult as you could throw at someone. He had been called it many times himself, mostly by bigger boys looking for someone to torment. He knew he didn't want to be 'one of the Bonnie kids' and was alarmed to hear it mentioned now.

"Why on earth would I do that? He's a perfectly normal boy who happens to have one leg shorter than the other and some burns, he's as bright as the next kid and I want him to come back to his school."

"Well, I can see you're determined about this. I'll make the arrangements for September – on your own head be it."

On the walk home he put his hand in his mums and let her hold it all the way home.

The following months were some of happiest of his short life so far. He had his mum's full and undivided attention as she tried to help him with his letters and numbers, so he wasn't too far behind when he went back. There was also time for playing out in their yard, trips out, wearing a newly purchased floppy hat that he detested but his mum assured him would protect him from the sun and stop people staring so much.

He enjoyed sunny days, shared snacks, meals at the kitchen table and time to play with his toys and practise his drawing skills under his mums encouraging and kindly tutorage. Once the summer holiday started, he was allowed out to play with the other children in the street as they chalked on the pavements and threw balls to each other. Under the vigilant supervision of his mum, who watched from the front step, he enjoyed spending time with the other kids and it helped fuel his excitement and anticipation for the Autumn and his return to school.

As the big day approached, he was kitted out with a new uniform, crisp and sharp from the shop in town. He practised wearing it around the house until his mum insisted he took it off and kept it clean for the first day. This couldn't come quickly enough for Chris, he counted the days, asked about what they would be doing at school, asked if the same kids would still be there, asked who his teacher would be, asked a hundred questions a day until September finally arrived and he walked proudly off with his mum (definitely not holding hands this time) to get some answers.

There was lots of staring at first, and lots of innocent questions as classmates started to get to know him again. Some of the previous difficulties of keeping up and joining in remained, but the classwork was easy for him after months of reading, writing and counting practise at home under the supervision of his mum. This endeared him to his teacher, Mrs Price, and offered him some protection when he was under her watchful, kindly eye. When he was not the combination of his appearance, his disability and the fact he was the teacher's pet, made him a target for the more vindictive and unprincipled members of the school community. Even some of the other teachers, including the headmistress, showed their fear of him by being indifferent at best, unkind at worst.

It was at this time Janet Cox came into his life. She was in the year below him, and had not been in the school when he was last there. It was one playtime, when she and her friends were doing their best to annoy him as he sat playing Top Trumps on a bench, that she came up with the nickname Quasimodo, to the general hilarity of all those around. The nickname stuck and the teasing continued and escalated as he progressed through the school. By the time he was at secondary school the bullying was daily, and more intense as his classmates, and in particular Janet Cox - who now only called him Bonnie Quasimodo, got older and crueller. Children who would be friends were also targeted and dropped away, leaving Chris lonely, isolated and angry.

That was how his school career progressed. He did well in his lessons, suffered in the playground, had few friends. Then there was prize day, Chris did not want to dwell on that, but afterwards he gradually spent more time feigning illness and staying at home. Or simply staying at home if his mum was at work. He preferred his own company to that of his tormentors and sat at home working through textbooks, writing and drawing and listening to loud, angry music.

CHAPTER 10

EVENING IN

The house was empty again. Polly had still not returned and Dave was his usual unpredictable self, who knew when he would get home. She stood, car keys in hand and coat still on, inside the front door momentarily. She listened to the silence of the house then turned around and walked back to the car, letting the door slam shut behind her.

She found herself sitting in the car just up the road from Chris's house. She could see his tidy front garden, neat rows of pots with flowers in bloom, and his red front door with its precisely painted house number clear and white. From where she sat, she could not look inside the house, and wasn't sure if she would try peering through the windows anyway. She wasn't even sure if she would be brave enough to knock on his door, she only wanted to check he was okay, let him know that someone was on his side. But she had never seen him outside of work apart from occasionally bumping into him in the supermarket or at drunken work parties, where he was usually the first to leave.

When she had started working at Potters he was already an established member of staff. At first she had been shocked and, if she was honest with herself, a little repulsed, by his appearance. But gradually she had come to know him, his quiet sense of humour and patient support when she got things wrong had been exactly what she needed to settle into her job. He was very private and it took a long time to tease out information about his life outside of work, or to wait for him to let slip pieces of information – not that she was fishing, but working closely with someone you expect to start to get to know them a little.

He always seemed very attentive to others, remembering the names of partners, children and other little pieces of information that meant he could have casual conversations comfortably with other staff. And by and large other staff were pleasant to him, nobody seeming to mind his appearance once the initial surprise of meeting him had worn off, until Lagrange. Lagrange had never seemed to be able to treat with Chris with any respect or have pleasant conversations with him, always on his case or asking him to do more and more. Chris took this stoically, and after the incident today Bev guessed that there was more to their strained relationship than just Chris's damaged exterior, Chris knew something that Lagrange didn't want him, or anybody else, to know.

And then there was Kiera. She was still shocked by what had happened, she had heard enough of the conversation to get the idea. She wanted to knock on the door and talk to Chris, tell him what she had done, tell him it was okay, tell him that everybody else thought he was okay – that they liked him and didn't judge him on his appearance. She wanted to try and comfort him, take away some of the anger and hurt she had seen clearly painted on his face that morning. But she was torn, she didn't want to intrude on his privacy that he was so protective of – she only knew his house because Jim, their old boss, had asked her to deliver his pay cheque to him once, when he had been unwell (this was in the old days, before everything got sent straight to the bank.)

"Would you mind, it's on your way home and I know Chris won't be able to pay it into his bank until next week otherwise."

She had just slid it through the letterbox and started to walk back to her car when the door opened and a smiling face had called to her;

"Thank you love, do you want to come in for a cuppa? I'm sure Chris would love to see you."

She wasn't sure if he would if he was feeling ill, and she needed to get going to collect Polly from the childminder and put the tea on.

Bev hadn't wanted to intrude then, and still didn't. She considered writing a note and paying a return visit to the letter box, she had found one of the many pens she kept stashed in her handbag but could not locate a piece of paper that wasn't a receipt or a shopping list. Also, she didn't really know what she would say, how to put into words the things that she wanted to say that would start to put things right.

As she rummaged, reminding herself to replace the notebook that she was certain she had kept in here somewhere, her phone pinged. It was Dave asking where she was. She messaged back to say she was on her way, had just popped out, and then put the car into gear and drove home.

Dave was upstairs when she got back, getting changed out of his work shirt, ready for a trip to the pub with his friends.

"I thought we were going to watch a film tonight?"

"Sorry, I forgot, maybe tomorrow, it's Doug's last night before he goes off to Dubai. Can't Polly watch it with you?"

"She's not here."

"I'll make it up to you. What's for tea?"

She wanted him to ask how her day had been, wanted him to ask so she could tell him what had happened. Maybe she hoped he would know what she should do, be able to offer some sort of suggestion for how she could help Chris. He didn't, he told her about his day while they ate the food she had prepared and then left 'don't want to keep everyone waiting', leaving her to clear up and spend the evening watching TV by herself again.

CHAPTER 11

NOT AGAIN - AGAIN

Chris checked his blog; the numbers had settled a bit now.

They were still growing slightly, but not as exponentially as they had earlier in the week. Clearly all his new readers would be expecting something new from Mr Angree soon, but not today. He had started to draft something about his day, but it didn't flow, it was still too raw and recent for him to write anything but an incoherent rant. After several attempts he gave up and put on some music instead.

No Radio 2 for him today; he delved into his record box and found some of the music that had helped him through his teens. No love songs or ballads had seemed to have been written for someone as unlovable as him. Instead he gravitated towards The Stranglers, Stiff Little Fingers, The Clash – music written in anger, music for outsiders and misfits. Music for him. The music his mum gave him the money to buy, then complained that he played it. The complaints were half-hearted though, more about the volume than the music itself.

Now he immersed himself in it once again, his refuge and retreat when he wanted to escape from the world around him. He found himself half singing, half shouting along with lyrics so familiar that he could keep one step ahead of the music, draw a breath ready for the chorus then blast out the words with gusto and venom. Knowing other people were angry and felt they didn't belong in the world validated his feelings. He wanted to put Kiera and Janet Cox out of his mind, but even his precious collection of vinyl records with their worn sleeves and familiar scratches and hisses couldn't do that.

Wanting to be doing something, he walked around to The Crown for a drink. Roger was busy when he arrived, serving the same young men who'd been there last time. Not just them either, they'd bought another friend along. They were laughing amongst themselves, seemingly oblivious to the surrounding oasis of calm and quietness. One of them, the one in the ripped skinny jeans and tracksuit top, topped off with a baseball cap, was loudly describing his weekend at some festival or other. (Apparently, it is possible to stay awake for 3 days and nights with the right combination of chemical assistance), and every female present had found him irresistible.

Chris made short work of his drink. He said goodnight to Roger, who raised his eyebrows and shrugged slightly as he glanced across at another roar of raucous laughter from the table by the fruit machine. Chris went back home and sat down at his computer. Even more pissed off now than he had been earlier he selected the most coherent of the lengthy rants he had written earlier in the evening, added a bit at the end about 'bloody kids taking over the pubs like they invented drinking', and posted it.

That night he lay in bed waiting. Enveloped in the darkness he watched the space under the desk, waiting for the red eyes to flicker into life and his nocturnal torment to begin. Gradually, with the events of the day running on continual loop inside his head, he started to fall asleep. His last thought before he gave in and let his eyes slide shut was; 'maybe not tonight, I just imagined it all after all.'

His next thought was; 'What the fuck….' As he was awoken by the sound of 'I'm an Upstart' blasting out of his speakers at a volume loud enough to awaken him abruptly.

"I'm an upstart, hey!! Whatcha gonna do?

I'm an upstart listen!! I'm talking to you!"

He looked over to the record player to see Poquelin sitting beside it looking at him. He had managed to create a Mohican effect by apparently reshaping the top of his oily black head into a peak somehow, rising up over his horns. In one of his pointed ears there was a shining safety pin attached and he had a thick chain with a padlock dangling from it around his neck. He looked somehow simultaneously intimidating and ridiculous. He was nodding his head vigorously and gave Chris a thumbs up as he looked in his direction.

"Groovy tune, right?" he shouted over the sound of the music.

"Switch it off."

"What?"

"Switch it off."

"Can't hear you," replied Poquelin, pointing towards the speakers.

Chris heaved himself out of bed and roughly knocked the stylus, sending it skidding across the record to land with an amplified 'clunk' on the edge of the turntable. He sat back heavily on the bed.

"What the fuck? I was sleeping."

"You're not now."

"No, I'm fucking not, what do you want?"

"You should have slapped her, then you should have found out where Janet Cox lives and gone round and slapped her too."

"What?"

"You should've slapped both of them, bastards!"

"Oh piss off, why would I slap anybody?"

"After what she said to you? After the way her mum bullied you when you were at school? Why would you not? Do you really think these things are just going to go away if you don't do something about it, if you don't deal with it?"

"I'm not going to slap anybody, and it did go away, for years. Until you appeared funnily enough. Why don't you just go away and let me sleep?"

Poquelin was unperturbed, "Well what are you going to do about it then? You can't just let it go. Maybe you should pay somebody else to do it, if you're not man enough to do it yourself. I bet those lads in the pub would burn down her house for 50 quid if you asked them."

"I'm not burning down anybody's house, or paying anybody else to do it, are you mad?"

"It has been said. But if that's not the plan what is? Wasn't it bad enough at school when she got her boyfriend to cut your tie in half, or when she chalked 'spastic' on the back of your blazer? Are you going to let her kid do the same things to you? Tch, and after you stood up for her and everything, some people have no manners."

"It might not have been her that chalked on my blazer." Chris replied sullenly.

"Really? Oh, come on, who are you kidding? You know full well it was her, and all the other things that, even if she didn't do them, she started them. She was the one who got the whole bullying thing rolling wasn't she? And what about Prize day? It seems like she's not done yet either. You need to do something."

"Well, maybe I should talk to her." It sounded weak even as he said it, and he knew he had no intention of ever voluntarily speaking to Janet Cox. Ideally, he would never set eyes on her again, that would suit him, had suited him for years. But now she was back, and he knew Poquelin was right, that he should do something, but probably not burning down her house.

"Talk to her, yes that would work."

"Do you think so, really?"

"Of course not, stupid. You really are a twat sometimes. 'Maybe I should talk to her'. Maybe you should buy her some flowers and invite her to a dance." He picked up the record from the turntable and threw it, like a frisbee, at Chris. Chris ducked just enough for it to skim the top of his head and clatter against the wall.

"Don't do that, that's an original, it's worth a lot."

"What, like this one?" Poquelin held up a Clash single, pulled it from its sleeve and flicked it in the same direction as the first one. This time Chris did not duck far enough and the record hit the palm of his hand that he had put up reflexively in front of his face. It fell to the floor where Chris bent to pick it up just as the Ramones flew past his head.

"Stop! Okay, seriously – what can I do that's not actually illegal and won't hurt anybody? Nothing. If I'm just careful I can stay away from them, that way nobody gets hurt."

"How did that work out last time?"

Chris thought of the time he had spent out of school, the loneliness and tedium of sitting at home while he knew the rest of the world was out enjoying themselves. It had been a lonely time. His mum had done her best to keep his spirits up, to let him know he was loved and that it didn't matter what he looked like. But in spite of what she said Chris knew in his heart that it did matter, that he would always be judged – and found wanting.

"Nobody got hurt."

"You did, it hurt you. For someone clever you're very stupid sometimes. You spent years shut in here, you're still here most of the time, complaining about things on this," he smacked the top of the computer monitor, "as if that's going to make anything better. Although…."

"Although what?" Chris asked, wishing almost immediately that he hadn't.

"Well, it's just a thought, but can't you find a way to get back at her using this? You understand the internets and everything, I'm sure someone as smart as you could cause some damage with this box of wires and whirry bits."

"Cause some damage? What, you mean troll her?"

"Not a phrase I'd use, have some respect. But yes, give her hell. Find her on here and make her life a misery."

"Ridiculous."

"Not as ridiculous as doing nothing, wimp."

"I'm not doing that; I'd be no better than her."

"But no worse. You need to hit back, you need to hit where it hurts. Poison her, make her life miserable, let people know what a bastard she is, spread rumours and lies about her. She'd do the same to you – hell, she already did. Remember the time she…"

"I'm not listening anymore, and I'm not doing it. Leave me alone, I'm going to sleep." He lay back down and covered himself up, closing his eyes and willing himself to sleep.

Much later he woke again. Poquelin was gone and the room was silent now, it was lit up by the glow of the computer screen. Chris looked over and saw it was open on Janet Cox's Facebook page, her smiling, over made-up, middle-aged face looking out into the bedroom.

CHAPTER 12

TAKE THE MORNING OFF

The toast popped up at the same time as the kettle finished boiling, leaving Chris with the dilemma of buttering it before it started to cool or leaving it for a moment while he wet his tea bag. He hated it when that happened but never seemed to be able to coordinate things properly. He opted for pouring the water on the teabag and leaving it to stew while he added butter and marmalade to the toast, which he started to eat while he finished making his tea. Afterwards he rinsed the cup and plate, left them on the draining board and went back upstairs. As he walked past the door of the front bedroom on his way to the bathroom, he opened it and looked into the cluttered but empty bedroom.

"Are you okay? do you need anything?"

"No, I might get up in a bit. I'll make myself a cup of tea when I'm downstairs."

He knew she wouldn't, she hadn't been out of bed for several days, apart from brief commutes to the loo. He humoured her anyway;

"Sure, do you want me to get your slippers and dressing gown ready for you?"

"Maybe in a minute. What are you up to today?"

"I'm off to work in a bit, Auntie Jean's coming to sit with you. I'll come back later, before the doctor comes round."

"There's no need for the doctor, I'll be right as rain in a couple of days. It's just a bug, you don't need to worry about me."

"Ok, well we'll see what the doctor says shall we? I'll bring you up a cup of tea, do you want some porridge or toast?"

"Oh, don't worry yourself, just the tea would be lovely." She tried to smile, but the effect on her thin face made it look more like a grimace, maybe it was – he knew she was hurting but not saying anything, trying to be stoic. He'd had to insist on making a call to the doctor in the end, despite all her protestations and claims of robust health and ambitions to be back on her feet. The receptionist had tried to protect the doctor's precious time and then tried to insist that a home visit would not be possible. Theappointment had been hard won and he was determined to be there for it, to make sure the doctor wasn't fooled by the claims of good health and denial of symptoms. She had hardly eaten for the last fortnight, when she thought he was out of earshot he heard her groan and wince. When he was present, she moved with gritted teeth and a pursed mouth as she tried to hide her pain from him. Now she had taken to her bed and stopped eating altogether.

"You've got the phone there, make sure you call if you need me to come back for anything won't you?" He knew she wouldn't, but there's always a first time for everything.

"Okay love, you'd better get going or you'll be late."

"See you this afternoon then, get some rest."

"Hah, get some rest! I've been in bed for days; I won't get much more rested than this."

It was true that she had been in bed, but also true that she had not been sleeping at night, he could hear her tossing and turning from his room. Every time her light went on or off, every time she coughed or knocked something down reaching for it, he was awake and listening waiting to see if he was needed. He still wasn't sure how it had got this bad this quickly, had he missed something? Did he have his eye off the ball? Or did it really go from good to bad in the blink of an eye?

"Well, you look after yourself. Jean's got the spare key, she'll let herself in, we're all worried about you. You need to look after yourself."

"I should be looking after you really, you've done so well, I'm proud of you you know?"

"I know you are; you don't need to worry about me, I'm doing fine."

"Are you? I know it hasn't been easy, I wish I could've done more to help you, you deserve it."

"You've done plenty to help me, you've always been there for me, always supported me."

"I wish I could've done more though."

He sensed she was going to cry; they had been over this more times than he could count. She blamed herself for what had happened to him, and all the subsequent pain and anguish. He had tried to reassure her that it was his own ambition outmatching his physical ability that had been the cause. Regardless, she still carried the burden of guilt and continued to struggle with her emotions whenever she looked at his twisted face, even all these long years later.

"I'll see you later, play nice with Auntie Jean and I'll be back for when the doctor gets here. I'm bringing up some yogurt with your cup of tea, try and eat some of it will you – you're wasting away. I don't want people to think I'm starving you."

"I'll eat some, I promise."

She wouldn't, but he took it up to her anyway, with her tea, and kissed her goodbye before he hurried off to work.

He really needed to start clearing the room out now, he could use the space as a hobby room, take some of the clutter out of his bedroom. Not today though. He was undecided whether to go into work. He didn't want to after yesterday, but a big delivery was due in and it didn't seem fair to leave Tim and Bev to deal with it by themselves. Not that they weren't capable, but Bev had her own job to do – and was still showing Janet Cox's bloody daughter the ropes. Tim could manage, but it would be quicker and easier if he was there to check everything off.

The delivery wasn't due until the afternoon. Chris made a decision, he would take the morning off – take it out of his annual leave, he still had loads of days left – and go to work in time to process the order. This way he would spend most of his time in the yard with Tim and minimise the amount of time he had to spend in the proximity of Kiera. This decided he went back to his room and sat down at the computer.

Janet Cox's face stared back at him, painted smile and dyed hair trying to reclaim some of the years she had lost. 'A least I never had any good looks for time to steal from me' he thought to himself, his fingers hovered over the keyboard as he decided what he should do next.

CHAPTER 13

IT'S GOING TO BE A LONG DAY

D ave was in the bath. Not 'having a bath', just in the bath; fully clothed and snoring with the towels pulled vaguely over him in a rough assimilation of blankets. She had heard him come home in the early hours of the morning, shouting goodbye to the taxi driver, tripping over the pots on the front garden as he cut across the lawn, trying (unsuccessfully) to tiptoe up the stairs, looking into the bedroom to check she was asleep, and finally throwing up in the toilet. She washed in the sink, brushed her teeth and used the toilet, none of it quietly, he did not stir. As she left the room she leaned over and turned the shower on, walking away from the ensuing noise and complaints.

She was in the kitchen drinking coffee and eating toast when Dave came in. He had a sheepish expression, tinged with nauseousness, as he came within smelling distance of Bev's breakfast. He had taken off his wet shirt and jumper and had a towel draped over his bare shoulders. Seeing him half dressed and hungover made Bev madder than she already was, she didn't know why, it just did.

"Nice night out then?"

"I'm sorry love, I really am."

"Three in the morning."

"Ooh, don't shout. It was Doug's last night."

"I'm not shouting, but I am going to need to apologise to the neighbours, probably to half the street. What were you thinking making all that racket? Number 23 have small children."

"I'm really sorry, I think we all just got carried away."

"How much did you spend?"

A pause; "Doug got most of them in, he's off to earn some tax-free money so he's feeling flash."

'Bloody liar' thought Bev, she was certain that it had been the intention all along for everybody to stay out late and drink copious amounts. She was also sure that Dave would have spent enough to have paid for a whole week's shopping, he was never shy when it came to getting rounds in. And now he was going to lose at least another half a day's pay on top of that.

"Go and sleep it off, you can't drive now, you'll still be drunk."

"No, I'm pretty sure I'll be…."

"No, you won't. You know as well as I do how long it takes. If you were still drinking at 2, and I guess you were, that was only 6 hours ago. If you lose your license, you'll probably lose your job, or worse still you might kill somebody. Go back to bed, sleep it off and go in at lunchtime."

Dave looked as if he was going to argue with her, he started to open his mouth, but closed it again when Bev looked at him with an expression that said 'God help me, if you say anything at all I will probably kill you.' He started to walk backwards to the stairs, crestfallen and hangdog.

"I'm really sorry love, I'll make it up to you."

"We'll talk about it."

Bev watched him turn and slink slowly back up the stairs, then cleared up her breakfast things, banging them into the sink and crashing them onto the draining board. She briefly considered giving the sitting room and hall a quick hoover, but decided that would be cutting her nose off to spite her face. Instead, she left early for work, planning to stop on the way and get a nice coffee, sod the expense, if they can afford nights out drinking till the early hours then they can afford a decent cup of sodding coffee.

When she got to work, she wasn't completely surprised to find a message from Chris saying he would be late in. She was surprised to find Kiera already there. She was quiet, and not really making eye contact with her, but she was there. Bev did not broach the subject of what had happened the day before, waiting instead for Kiera to say something about it. It was a long time coming and certainly not worth the wait. A momentary lull in activity left the two of them standing quiet and alone for the first time that morning. Keira looked at Bev, for a moment she thought she wouldn't say anything, as she worked up the courage to say what was on her mind. Then, in a rush to get the words out before she lost her nerve or forgot them, she reached up and held the end of her hair – twisting it around her finger, and started;

"My mum said he got her into loads of trouble when they were at school. She said he was always bunking off and that he pestered the girls."

Bev didn't know how to respond, she had expected some kind of an apology, or some measure of remorse. Instead, here was Kiera doubling down on her behaviour.

"Maybe that's true, or maybe it was thirty-five years ago, I don't know because I didn't know Chris when he was at school. I do know that in all the years I've known him he's never got anyone in trouble, pestered anyone or caused any kind of problems."

"Yeah, well my mum said...."

Bev interrupted;

"One of the things about having a job and being at work is that your mum isn't here. You need to make your own choices and decisions about how you talk to people and treat them, and how you spoke to Chris yesterday was wrong. When you get to know him you may like him, most people do, or you may not. But you shouldn't not like him just because he looks different and your mum doesn't like him."

"I just thought…. I dunno, he does look kind of creepy and like, you know…."

Kiera was flushed now, the lock of hair in her hand was being twisted furiously and her expression was confused, clearly she did not want to give ground, she was used to being right, even when she was wrong. Bev saw a glimmer of confusion in her eyes and thought how she might have handled a situation like this with Polly, not that her own daughter had ever presented her with a situation precisely like this.

"You know, I found it confusing when I first started work. You don't really know who does what – or what they expect you to do. And you had an awful first day with that incident with Mr Lagrange, that must have been dreadful for you. But once you get to know everyone and find your feet you realise it's all just a big family really."

Kiera grunted and continued to twiddle with her hair.

"Chris is going to be in later today, you could always try talking to him, maybe get to know him a bit."

From the look on Kiera's face, this was clearly not something she wanted to do. Nevertheless, she grunted again, looked down at the floor and said;

"S'pose."

Bev took that as a positive and encouraging step forward and turned to help the customer who had just approached the counter, she smiled and simultaneously groaned inwardly – it had already been a long day and there was still quite a lot of it left to go.

Chris arrived around lunch time, he limped in and collected some paperwork then went straight out to the yard, presumably to find Tim. He gave Bev a cursory smile and nod hello on his way past, he looked strained and tired. Bev guessed they all did today, Chris was still upset, Kiera was conflicted and she was torn between the two of them, and troubled by thoughts of what she would say to her idiot husband later. Lagrange continued to hide in his office, making only occasional forays into the main building before scampering back into his hidey hole.

CHAPTER 14

OUT WITH THE OLD

Once the deliveries started to arrive and Tim got busy checking everything off, Chris became too busy to think about anything much apart from numbers of pallets, quality of plants and making sure everything was stacked ready for the team to get it all out in the correct places as quickly as possible.

In snatched moments between flurries of activity Tim shared a small black and white picture of an ill-defined, poorly focussed embryo. Squinting, Chris could follow Tim's direction and recognise the head and the back and fledgling limbs. What Chris could not fail to see was Tim's evident pride, excitement and nervousness. He cooed over the picture and, in spite of having no experience of it himself, talked about what a fantastic adventure it would be to embark on the journey of parenthood.

The words appeared well-judged, as Tim started to talk about the preparations they were making; painting the nursery, choosing a buggy, buying a cot. The list of things needed to successfully care for a small human seemed extraordinary, everything big people needed and more - but smaller and cleaner. Chris made a mental note to get Tim and Deb a Mothercare gift card for his leaving present.

The afternoon flew by, and Chris ended up back in his office filing all the paperwork and squaring up all the invoices and delivery notes. While he wouldn't exactly say he enjoyed doing this, he did find it absorbing as he methodically worked his way through each task and made everything tally up. The remainder of the afternoon passed quickly. At one point his office door opened, he looked up expecting it to be Bev and was surprised and a little unnerved to see Kiera standing there with a mug of tea.

"Bev asked me to pop this in to you."

She found it hard to make eye contact with him and was clearly speaking through gritted teeth. For his part it was all Chris could do to take the mug from her and mumble 'thanks' before carrying on with his work. He was pretty sure this was Bev's attempt at arbitration, he didn't want to offend her by blowing it straight away, but he had no idea how he was going to manage to work with Janet Cox's daughter day in and day out.

As often happens at the end of a busy day, synchronicity kicks in and everybody leaves at the same time, especially when everybody has been unloading and stacking a huge start of season order. Chris moved out with everybody else, walking alongside Tim, who subconsciously slowed down to allow for the difference in their step size caused by Chris's lurching, lopsided gait. He was talking about his plans for the house and when and where his leaving party would be.

Chris was half listening, he saw Bev getting into her car and thought she looked preoccupied, she didn't give him a wave, didn't even seem to notice him and Tim as she drove past. He wished he had found time to talk to her during the day, but he had been busy; also, he hadn't wanted to see Kiera any more than he absolutely had to. He hoped Bev didn't think he had been avoiding her. Tim said goodbye and got into his car as Chris walked the extra distance to his own, his penance for arriving late was that he had to park at the far end of the staff car park. A price worth paying in his mind.

There was another car parked next to his own, one he didn't recognise from the familiar selection of staff vehicles that he usually saw. It was a bright blue hatchback with a selection of boy racer modifications; lowered suspension, coloured alloy wheels, oversized spoilers and coloured glass on the light clusters. The sort of car you see outside Halfords with groups of teenage boys gathered around comparing notes and listening to the stereo pumping out what Chris thought of condescendingly as 'Radio 1' music. Everything about it screamed 'tasteless' to Chris, the driver was revving the engine loudly as the passenger door was shutting.

As the car roared again it span its wheels and shot out of its space, Chris saw that the person in the passenger seat was Kiera. She was still doing her seatbelt up and didn't look in his direction as she sped past, with heavy bass pumping loud enough to hear from outside the car, Chris was glad. He also caught a glimpse of the young man driving, he couldn't be certain but he thought he recognised him in the brief time he had sight of him. He walked on to his own car trying to think where he would know him from. As he unlocked his car and lowered himself into the driver's seat it hit him, one of the lads who had recently invaded the Crown with his loud and lairy mates. Of course Kiera would know them, why wouldn't Janet Cox's daughter be driving around with the local louts.

Chris's car was of an age where it still sported a cassette player. He rummaged around and found a tape he had made with a selection of suitably distracting music, mostly rockabilly; the Cramps and the Meteors featured heavily. He turned it up as he drove home trying to plan how he could still go to work and not actually have to speak to Kiera. Maybe he was being unfair, maybe her bringing him tea was a genuine attempt at reconciliation. He didn't think so, but he was willing to give her the benefit of the doubt and give it a go. The thought of it made him feel sick, but he knew it was the right thing to do. It was definitely what Bev would want him to do.

He pulled up outside the house with Repo Man just coming to an end, a suitable song for the day, and went inside.

"Is that you love?"

"No, burglars, how are you?"

"I'm fine, I'll get going now you're home."

"You don't need to rush off you know."

"My bus is in 10 minutes, I don't want to miss it."

"I can give you a lift if you want."

"No, that's okay, I've got my bus pass."

"Well, if you're sure. How's she been?"

"Mostly asleep, I persuaded her to have a bit of soup at lunchtime. She didn't have much of it though. The nurse came to check on her, said there wasn't anything she needed to do today."

"Thanks Auntie Jean, you're a star. How's Tom getting on?"

"He's doing fine, he likes his new job. Says they're not as friendly there, not that he remembers to ring very often. I think he's busy with his new girlfriend."

"Well at least he's found one friendly person then. Is he coming home soon?"

"He said he'd try and get back for before Christmas, maybe he'll bring his new friend with him. I'll tell him to pop in and say hello if he does."

"I'm sure he'll have better things to do, but say hello to him from me won't you."

"I will do, I'm looking forward to seeing him and he's not been gone long. How silly am I?"

Jean bustled around pouring her belongings back from the table into her oversized handbag; a crossword book, some knitting, a packet of mints and a Mill's and Boon paperback. As she walked to the door Chris asked again;

"Sure you don't want a lift? It won't take a minute."

"No, you go on upstairs and see how she is. I'll let myself out, see you tomorrow."

"Okay, thanks again. Have a good evening."

She left, pulling the door shut behind her, leaving Chris to go upstairs and see how everything was. Her eyes were open and she was sipping some water when he went in.

"Hello love, has Jean gone?"

"Yes, just left. She'll be back tomorrow. How are you feeling?"

"So so, I might sit in my chair for a bit. Do you want to watch TV with me?"

Chris helped her out of bed and into the armchair he had bought upstairs into the room and sat and watched the news with her on the small TV he had rigged up in the corner of the room. She had fallen asleep again by the time it got to the local news, he covered her gently with a blanket and kissed her gently on the forehead.

Looking around the room now he decided he should make a start with the clearing out. He got all the clothes from the wardrobe and chest of drawers and laid them on the bed. The smells and colours transporting him back to familiar times and places – reminding him of her. This was the dress she'd worn that warm summer night that they went to the concert in the park, her 'best' dress. Her favourite blue cardigan that she liked to sit and watch TV in, the frayed and worn gardening shirt that always went with her big straw hat that he now lifted down from the top of the wardrobe. All of his memories of her life encapsulated in a collection of worthless clothes.

Now all the clothes were out he wasn't sure what to do with them. He considered for a moment, then went downstairs and bought back a roll of bin bags that he started to fill one by one until they formed a collection of bags in a pyramid by the door. Next, he got a cardboard box from the cupboard, he slowly started to fill it with ornaments and nick-nacks from around the room. He stopped to look at things as he went, it didn't occur to him that anything might have monetary value, they were just ornaments and keepsakes. Soon the box was full and the surfaces were mostly empty, some of the pictures he had left on the ledges, the rest could go with the clothes to a charity shop. Tomorrow was his day off, he would see if he could take it all then and get it done.

As he was leaving the room, preoccupied with wondering how many of the bags would fit in his car, he brushed past a photo frame that he had placed too near the edge of the surface it occupied.

Before he was able to stop it the frame tumbled to the floor and the glass broke with a dull cracking sound. He bent to pick it up and saw that it was a picture of her dad – grandad John, smiling as he stood outside the front door of a small terraced house. He was wearing a cap and his second-best jacket and tie, cigarette in hand and looking like he was on his way out somewhere.

Chris carefully scooped up the pieces of broken glass and took the picture out of the modest silver frame, hoping it wasn't damaged. As he removed it a small piece of paper fell out and fluttered to the floor. Picking it up he saw it was an old bus ticket, he turned it over and there on the back in faded blue ink was the autograph that Norman Wisdom had signed for her when they went to see him filming. Chris sat heavily on the edge of the bed, looking at the ticket through blurry tear-filled eyes.

CHAPTER 15

NEW ZEALAND

There was a holdall on the floor in the hallway when Bev let herself in. It was Polly's, she must have come back to do some laundry. Bev called her name and got a muffled response from upstairs.

"I'll put the kettle on," she shouted back.

Polly came into the kitchen as she was pouring the hot water into the mugs. She put her bag by the washing machine, best to do these things in increments, and came over and gave Bev a hug.

"Hi mum, how are you?"

"I'm fine, how about you? I haven't seen you for ages."

She looked at her daughter, dressed in a pair of ripped jeans and trainers with a grey jumper and her long dark hair tied back, she was growing up fast. No – had grown up, very much a young woman now, making Bev wonder where all the years had gone.

"Well, a few days Mum – don't exaggerate. I've been busy with my assignment for uni, it's all go with finals coming up this year. How's dad?"

"In disgrace, he was out drinking 'till the early hours last night. He woke up half the street coming home then threw up in the bathroom and slept in the bath."

Polly barely supressed a giggle, she took her mug and fished the teabag out as she asked; "Did he still get up for work?"

"Eventually, he looked like death this morning."

"Isn't he a bit old for that really? That's the sort of thing I'm supposed to be doing, only I'm not because I have so much work to hand in."

"Yes, he is too old for that really. What work have you got to get done?"

"Just an assignment, but it's taking me ages, there's so much research for it. I've nearly broken the back of it now though."

"That's good, anything I can do to help?"

Polly looked down at her holdall and then back up at her mum with a sheepish expression and half a smile.

"Of course, leave it with me. Are you staying for tea?"

"What is it?"

"I was going to make a risotto, although I don't know how much your dad will want, I expect he's still feeling green around the gills."

She had been going to bake a potato and have it loaded with cheese and beans, but knew that risotto was Polly's favourite. It was a blatant and brazen attempt to try and persuade Polly to stay. It worked.

"I'd love to, but I need to go back out at 7, I'm meeting a friend to go over the assignment, we've gone half and half on the research. Hopefully we'll both have the bits each other need to get it finished."

"That's not a problem, I'll start getting it ready now. Your dad will be pleased to see you."

It turned out he wasn't. Bev and Polly did laundry, cooked, drank tea and chatted in the kitchen. When Dave came in he looked dreadful, he stopped in the kitchen long enough to get a cup of tea and ascertain that everyone was okay, then announced;

95

"I feel like shit and I'm knackered, anyone mind if I go and lie down for half an hour."

Before he found out whether anyone minded or not he left the kitchen and his footsteps bumped their way up the stairs and into the bedroom, closing the door behind them. Polly giggled and Bev rolled her eyes, they dished up their own tea and left some covered on the side for when Dave reappeared. Bev was not sure they would see him again that evening, or that his food would get eaten.

Over the meal Polly made an announcement;

"I've decided to go travelling next year, I've saved enough for tickets to get to New Zealand and I've got a friend there who can help me out if I need it. Would you and dad be able to lend me some if I need a bit extra?"

Bev was taken by surprise; it had never occurred to her that her baby would want to go half way round the world on her own. She didn't know how she felt, what with Polly only being out of primary school such a seemingly short span of time ago.

"Who are you going with?"

"It was going to be a few of us, the others have all backed out. I still really want to go though; I don't know when I'll get another chance. I'll be looking for jobs and flats when I come back, I don't want to start doing that before I'd done something. There are farms where you can stay and work for food and a bed, it's all properly organised and everything."

Bev didn't know what to think. She was scared she was losing her daughter, scared of the potential danger she would be in travelling alone across the globe. Also, she was jealous. All her life she had wanted to travel, to have an adventure of her own and see the world, this had never happened; life got in the way. Now Polly was planning to go and see the world and Bev was still going to be stuck here, cooking and cleaning after Dave and working at the garden centre. It wasn't fair, but it was right. She looked at Polly, grown up, with an empty bowl in front of her and a glass of blackcurrant juice (Bev kept some in the cupboard for when she was at home.) Minutes before she couldn't imagine her going, now she couldn't imagine her not going.

"Of course. I'll talk to your dad when he's alive again, we can go half on your ticket if you want."

It was an executive decision; she would tell Dave that was what they were doing and he could like it or lump it. She had some money she had put to one side in the hope of going on holiday some time, and if they could afford for him to go out drinking and playing golf, they could afford for their only daughter to have the experience of a lifetime. Polly practically ran around the table, beaming she wrapped Bev in a big hug and thanked her profusely, she hugged her and smiled in a way Bev couldn't remember her doing for years. She knew then that she had done the right thing. The look on her face made it worth it, every penny. As for the risk and potential danger of the enterprise, didn't they bring their daughter up in the hope that she would be independent and smart? Hadn't they succeeded in this? The fact that she was even planning an expedition of this magnitude should be answer enough for that.

CHAPTER 16

THE CROWN

The Crown was quiet. Roger looked across the bar at the mostly empty tables. His eyes tracked to the only busy table, in the far corner. The lads were sat there again, two more of them tonight. They talked in hushed voices, occasional bursts of laughter and trips to the toilet or the bar, interspersed with smoke breaks on the front doorstep. Their interactions with him were brief and on the polite side of standoffish - just. Whatever it was they did, they could afford new phones and new-looking sportswear, the kind you see all the kids wearing nowadays, all padded and nylon.

He didn't know where any of them worked, but they never appeared to be short of cash. Honestly, he didn't mind that much as they were spending a good amount of it in his pub. He wondered if now might be the time to start expanding, draw in a younger crowd, maybe see if it would be possible to start doing some food, redecorate a bit, get a bigger TV than the portable one that currently sat behind the bar and only got switched on for special occasions.

Of course, he didn't want to upset his regulars. But they were hardly the last of the big spenders, and he had to make a living, didn't he? He wondered how they would react if he started making changes, if more of the local youngsters started coming in. Not the young youngsters obviously – he didn't want to lose his license, did he?

His eyes wandered back over to the group as he stood unloading the glass washer and stacking the glasses on the shelves. Another burst of raucous laughter, accompanied by some loud expletives, erupted from the corner. Roger smiled, shook his head and put the final glass on the shelf. He turned around and started to check which bottles needed replacing in the fridge.

CHAPTER 17

OVERKILL

C hris typed;

YES – CAPS LOCK IS ON! STRAP YOURELVES IN, I'M NOT JUST ANGRY TODAY – I'M FUCKING FURIOUS. STOP ME IF YOU'VE HEARD THIS ONE, THERE WAS THIS PERSON I WENT TO SCHOOL WITH – LET'S CALL HER 'TWAT A'. SHE WAS A COMPLETE AND UTTER TWAT, TOO SELF-CENTRED AND UP HERSELF TO EVER NOTICE ANYBODY ELSE EXISTED UNLESS IT WAS TO GET SOMETHING FROM THEM. OR BE SHITTY TO THEM ANYWAY, IT TURNS OUT THAT 'TWAT A' GREW UP AND WENT ON TO HAVE LITTLE TWATS OF HER OWN. I DON'T GIVE A RAT'S ARSE, SHE CAN DO WHAT THE FUCK SHE WANTS AS LONG AS I DON'T HAVE TO SEE HER BOVINE FACE OR LISTEN TO HER WHINING TWADDLE.

EXCEPT…ONE OF HER TWAT CHILDREN - 'TWAT B' – TURNED UP IN MY OFFICE THIS WEEK, AND IT APPEARS I'M GOING TO BE WORKING WITH HER. DEEP BREATH, PERHAPS THE APPLE FELL AWAY FROM THE TREE. DID IT FUCK? TURNS OUT SHE HAS BEEN WELL TRAINED IN

TWATISHNESS BY HER TWAT MOTHER. IN FACT, SHE MANAGED TO MAKE A COMPLETE TWAT OF HERSELF ON HER VERY FIRST DAY.

NORMALLY I WOULDN'T CARE LESS. BUT SOMEHOW IT HAS BEEN TURNED INTO ME BEING A TWAT. I MEAN, I AM, BUT I DON'T TRY AND FUCK THINGS UP FOR OTHER PEOPLE - WELL, NOT USUALLY ANYWAY.

SO NOW I HAVE TO SEE HER OVER MADE-UP FACE AND CALF-LIKE FEATURES EVERY TIME I GO TO WORK. FUCKING HELL, GIVE ME A BREAK WILL YOU. COMBINED WITH TWAT BOSS I FEEL LIKE I'M GOING TO SOME KIND OF TWAT REHAB CENTRE EVERY DAY.

I HAVE NO IDEA WHAT'S GOING TO HAPPEN NEXT, AFTER THIS I WOULDN'T BE SURPRISED IF THERE WAS A BIBLICAL PLAGUE OF LOCUSTS OR I GOT THE BLOODY SMALLPOX OR SOMETHING, THE HEAVENS HAVE TRULY OPENED AND LET LOOSE A STREAM OF RANCID PISS ON ME – AND I'M FURIOUS.

IF ANYBODY WANTS TO SUGGEST HOW I CAN MAKE SOME SENSE OF THIS SHITSHOW PLEASE LEAVE A MESSAGE IN THE COMMENTS SECTION. I PROBABLY WON'T ANSWER ANY OF THEM AS I'M SURE YOU ARE ALL AS TWATTISH AS THE TWATS I'M SURROUNDED BY. BUT FEEL FREE TO DO IT ANYWAY.

Chris clicked the submit button and got up from the desk. His eyes felt sore from sitting and reading through the ever-expanding list of comments and suggestions that had been left for on his previous post. They had stopped even the pretence of being polite now, obscene, virulent and frequently funny. The first response to his latest musing pinged up before he had even stood up;

'Bit rude. Give them hell.'

Chris briefly wondered if he should still be doing this, given the increasing numbers of weirdos and lunatics he appeared to be attracting amongst the web tourists who dropped by. But fuck it, he enjoyed writing it and it wasn't his responsibility who read it - was it?

He looked in the other bedroom, now stripped of its personality, and felt a pang of guilt – that he had taken away something that had belonged to someone else, violated their personal and private – albeit abandoned - space. The pragmatist in him knew that if he hadn't done it now, he would have just been putting off the inevitable. Knowing that did not make it easier. The bare mattress, empty drawers and cupboards and ledges and shelves with their paint sun-faded with the shapes and patterns of their previous occupants, all accused him of forgetting – or at least not caring enough to remember. Briefly he considered unpacking the boxes and bags and putting everything back in its proper place, rehanging the clothes, refilling drawers and arranging the shelves. Instead, he went downstairs and made a cup of tea, which he took to the lounge where he sat and watched TV. He knew he was doing the right thing, what else was he supposed to do? But it hurt. To make it worse, he was now sitting downstairs pretending he wasn't tired, so he could procrastinate and put off the moment he had to go to bed and be reawaken by Poquelin.

Later he opened his eyes, he was stiff from having fallen asleep in the armchair and badly needed to pee. The room was bathed in the bluish glow of the light from the TV, everywhere else was full dark and silent apart from the reassuring murmur of the teleshopping lady extolling the virtues of a kitchen gadget that bore more than a passing resemblance to a medieval torture implement he had seen a picture of in a book once. Best of all, it could be his for only £29.99, complete with every attachment and fitting he would ever need – to grate, mix, blend, slice and stir the entire contents of his kitchen.

"What a load of tat" he muttered to himself as he stood up and stretched.

"Pile of shite."

He turned around and there was Poquelin, leaning in the doorway.

"I waited upstairs, where were you?"

"Sod off."

Chris walked past him and up the stairs to the bathroom. Poquelin turned and followed two steps behind him, flapping and jumping a little to ensure they remained equidistant. He stood behind Chris and waited while he relieved himself, then hopped aside as he flushed and walked to the bedroom. As Chris started to change into his pyjamas Poquelin stood with his hands on his hips and his head tilted to one side.

"Well?"

"Well what?"

"Well, are you going to apologise?"

"What?"

"A-POL- O – GISE."

"What for?"

"Because I was right."

Chris climbed into bed and watched as Poquelin perched himself at the foot of the bed, facing him. He didn't know how such a misshapen, tusked, fiery eyed face could look smug, but it did.

"What the fuck are you on about?"

"I was right, you needed to do something instead of this wishy-washy liberal bollocks. Remind me, how did it work out?"

"I don't want to talk about it."

"You don't need to; you just need to admit I was right."

"You aren't right, you'll never be right. If I can't be better than them I might as well be nothing, I've got standards."

"You've got shafted – by everyone."

"Piss off."

"You need to do something; I've got a plan."

Poquelin tried to rearrange his features into something that resembled thoughtfulness and concern. He didn't succeed, but did manage to convey some kind of earnestness which annoyed and intrigued Chris in equal measures.

"A plan?"

"Yes."

"You've got a plan?"

"Yes."

That improbable smug look again, he crossed his legs and folded his arms – making him look for all the world as if he had tied himself in a knot. He waited patiently.

"I don't want to know what your plan is, I'm not interested."

"You do, it's a doozy."

"It will be as cruel and unpleasant as everything else you've said and done since I met you….or since you intruded into my life and home to be more accurate."

"Yeah, your perfect life. Get a grip, can't you see that sometimes you have to be firm. You have to stand up for yourself. You have to take action."

"I'm not interested in your plan."

Chris turned and switched off the light, then lay back down.

"I know you don't, but I'm going to tell you it anyway."

"I thought you might. Do what you need to do, I'm going to sleep."

"You see, you have a blog with hundreds of readers, or is it thousands now? Anyway, whatever, you also have the Facebook details of…."

Poquelin continued to drip poison into Chris's ear as he slid off into sleep. His body seemed to shine, even through its blackness and the dark of the night, as he sat on the bed like a parent comforting a child who has had a bad dream.

Chris did dream, he relived his years of pain and torment, he dreamed he was whole and strode like a colossus through streets crowded with people from his life. In his dream he was an important man, a man that people cared about what he thought and listened to what he said. He saw his mum waiting for him at the end of the busy street, she beckoned him forward and he hurried to her excitedly – no dragging foot to hold him up here, he ran to where she was waiting.

As he got closer, she started to morph, her features becoming less her, her age fluctuating and the clothes she was wearing cycling through a selection of outfits made from the clothes he recently removed from her wardrobe. Finally, as he approached the last stretch of the interminably long road, she settled on a blue skirt and blazer over a white blouse and striped tie. Her face settled into the mocking sneer of a teenaged Janet Cox, and abruptly it was prize day. Chris woke with sweat sheening his forehead in the first light of dawn. Knowing that sleep was over for the night he went downstairs and made himself a cup of tea as he tried to shake off the dream and start preparing for his day.

CHAPTER 18

BECAUSE IT'S MINE

T he other side of the bed was empty. Dave had slept on the couch and Bev had mostly lain awake thinking, trying to work out how a conversation about Polly had turned into a row that ended in tears and recriminations.

She thought his hangover had probably been a contributory factor, her underlying irritation about his previous nights' exploits had probably not helped in the end either. But she had started out with hope and expectation; hope that he would agree with her about giving Polly the money, and expectation that he would want to do what was best for his only daughter.

His immediate reluctance and hesitation had, in turn, made her defensive and a little angry. Didn't Polly deserve to have something nice? To give her something she would remember all her life? Wasn't this a chance to bridge a divide that had been opening between them and Polly before it became a chasm? Didn't he want to give her something they had never had? The more she had argued her case, the more Dave had dug in. Then Bev had done something she had never done before;

"Can we go through the bank statements together, to see how much we can afford? See if we can make some savings?"

"I keep an eye on the money, it's fine."

It was true, Dave had always been in charge of the money, ever since she had taken out a HP agreement for a new sofa when they were first married. He had gone ballistic, telling her they couldn't afford it and that she didn't understand it. Since then he had taken control, telling her how much they could spend and handing out cheques and sums of money when they were needed.

"I know you do, but maybe if we…."

"Maybe not. There's no need, I know how much we've got and we can't afford it."

"I'd really like to look."

"Don't you trust me then?"

"No, it's not that, but it's our money and I want to see what we can afford."

"It's not 'our' money, it's mine. I earn it and keep track of it. Don't I give you enough?"

"It's not that at all. I told you, I just want to look, I pay into it too."

"What, with your pin money job? I earn the proper money and I can look after it. I'm not giving all our money to Polly to piss away on beer, holidays and clothes."

"That's not what it's for - and it's both our money."

The conversation was becoming more animated as Bev became more frustrated and Dave more defensive. He stood up and put his hands on the table next to his untouched cup of tea that Bev had made for him. He was flushed and trembling slightly.

"I need a drink, I'm going out."

"So it's alright for you to piss away our money on beer then?"

"Yes, because it's MY money that I go out and work for every day."

He left the room, leaving Bev sitting alone, confused and angry. She heard the front door close, finished her own cup of tea and took both mugs to the sink and rinsed them out. She stood for a moment and looked out at the garden, neatly mowed lawn and a small shed. Decisively she went out to the shed and rummaged in the toolkit looking for the biggest, most robust screwdriver she could find. She took it into Dave's little study and started to pry at the locked desk drawer. It was not as easy as they make it look on films and TV shows, she slipped once and was lucky not to impale herself on the implement. But in the end the lock cracked and splintered, and the drawer grated open past the jagged wooden teeth-like shards. She took out the folders with 'pay slips' and 'bank statements' written on their spines in Dave's fussy, precise handwriting.

The extent of the deceit had staggered her, the lies by omission – and the outright lies - as she started to trawl through the carefully sorted and filed sheaves of paper. While she had been paying a share of the mortgage from her modest earnings, scrimping to stay on budget for food and essentials and try to keep some to one side for clothes, bills and car repairs, Dave had been living a different lifestyle altogether.

There were successive pay rises that he had not told her about, bonusses he had not mentioned – big bonusses. The golf clubs that he told her where a bargain weren't, and the golf club fees were nowhere near the small amount he had suggested when she had asked if they could afford it. Restaurant bills featured regularly – she could hear him in her head as he put the card on the table, 'it's okay, I've got this.' His suit was not an off the peg, she thought it had looked too nice for that. Scanning the statements, she came across one to a jeweller, £200. He had never bought her jewellery, preferring instead small bunches of flowers from the petrol station and chocolates - that he helped himself to as soon as they were opened. Her finger kept tracking back to that payment and a million questions pushed through her mind, questions that she could think of no answers for – except ones she didn't want to think.

Bev cried. Not loud sobbing tears, but a stream of hot water running silently down her face. She left the heaps of paper, with its miasma of numbers, spread across the table and went to bed where she lay silently with her questions playing in a loop in her head.

Later she heard the front door open and Dave clattering and bumping around the house. There was a pause, silence, then the thumping of footsteps on the stairs. The bedroom door banged open against the chest of drawers and Dave stood silhouetted in the doorway.

"You had no fucking right to go through my stuff."

Bev didn't answer.

"It's personal, it's my stuff."

Still no answer.

"It's my fucking money, I work hard for it, it's none of your fucking business what I spend my own fucking money on."

Silence. Dave slammed the door shut and crashed his way back downstairs. Bev cried.

Now Bev lay in bed, waiting until she heard Dave leave the house. Once she was sure he had gone she washed, dressed and went downstairs to get her breakfast before she left for work herself. The kitchen table had been cleared of the incriminating documents, the drawer was still open and empty, so she could only guess that Dave had taken the folders with him. She tidied the mess of blankets that had been left strewn around the sofa.

With all the changes at work, the stress with Kiera and Chris, and now this, she felt that life was ganging up on her. She thought of calling Polly, but didn't know what she might say to her.

"Hi Polly, sorry to wake you so early, but I wanted to talk to you about how your dad says we can't afford to help you out even though he seems to be living a life of luxury while I struggle to make ends meet. Oh, and I think he might be having an affair too."

Maybe not the best way to start Polly's day, or the way to build on their new-found common ground. Besides, didn't she say she had a university deadline looming? But if not Polly who? Bev had not been good at keeping up her friendships over the years, she had been busy being a mum, busy being a wife, busy going to work. Besides, there had been no money spare for fripperies like socialising or joining things. Except there had, just not for her. Now she had been forced to think about it, had she really not had time for those friendships, or had Dave gently dissuaded her from having interests outside the home?

"It's a bit tight this month love, can't we wait 'till we've changed the car?"

"I'd love for you to, but why don't we wait 'till after Christmas and see how we're doing?"

Always an excuse, always reasonable, for why she shouldn't do something.

She tidied away her breakfast debris, leaving the kitchen clean and tidy, the way Dave liked it, and went out to her car. Her cheap, functional car that Dave had chosen for her. She drove to work, the job that Dave had tried his best to dissuade her from taking,

"I just don't want you to look a fool when you realise that it's too much for you."

"You'll pay more in tax than you'll earn."

She settled into the routine of the day. It was Chris's day off today; Bev knew he would have noticed how preoccupied she was if he was here. He would have tried to give her a reason to smile, or offered some subtle distraction. His absence added to her unhappiness as she patiently explained things to Kiera, who was too self-absorbed to notice anything about anybody else. In fairness, she had been a quick learner and was getting the hang of things confidently. Soon she would know enough of the routine to be able to be left on her own more and the rota could start to get back to normal, she would have to remember to talk to Chris about that.

Lagrange was starting to venture from his office more now, getting back to his previous, irritating self. Moving things fractions of centimetres from where they had been placed, radioing people to ask them to do things they were already doing, avoiding customers. Bev genuinely couldn't see what it was that he actually contributed to the running of the centre sometimes. Still, hers not to reason why. She answered the phone as Kiera went over to the tills to cover one of the team for a break, she watched her and tried to see the confident and capable work colleague instead of the person who had unsettled her workplace and upset her friend.

She still did not fully understand what had gone on between her and Chris, but she had seen enough to know that the real problem was caused by someone who hadn't even been there. She didn't understand why or how yet, but she had her ideas. She had also seen enough to make her realise how much Chris had become an important part of her life, his ready smile, slightly shy diffidence and general helpfulness, so much so that she forgot sometimes how other people might perceive him. She did not always notice the faded scars on his face, and the limp was just a part of who he was. She wondered if he realised how little she or Tim, or any of their other workmates cared about his appearance, or how much they valued his friendship. Now she had been forced to really think about it, probably not. It was not the sort of thing she would say to someone, good old British reserve – not saying what we want to say because it's 'not done.'

All of these thoughts rattled along in tandem with her confusion and frustration over Dave's behaviour. She had called and texted his mobile, suggesting they needed to talk, but so far he had not responded. She didn't really want to talk to him right now, she felt scared and a little sick, but she knew it needed to happen. The money he had been spending, that she had not even known he was earning, the trouble he had gone to lie to her and deceive her. She thought of the opportunities that Polly had missed out on, because they were so hard up. Then there was the jewellers, who the hell had he been buying jewels for? Himself? Maybe a new watch or something. She felt sure she would have noticed something like that, but then again maybe she wouldn't, given how stupid she'd been for years.

She went through the day on autopilot as her mind ran through different permutations and possibilities for how the conversation might go. But as they day ended and she walked across the car park

111

beside Kiera, Dave had still not replied to her messages. She unlocked her car and got in as she waved to Kiera who sped off in her boyfriend's ludicrous, pimped-up car. She sat for a moment looking at her phone, wanting there to be a message and not wanting it at the same time. Her heart was in her mouth as she parked outside her house, unsure of what would be waiting inside, what kind of mood Dave would be in. Would he be remorseful and apologetic, or angry like he had been last night? She felt like she didn't really know who he was right now, and with that uncertainty came an edge of fear that she had not known around Dave before.

In the event it was neither. The house was exactly as she had left it that morning, two mugs on the draining board, folded blankets on the couch, a lonely emptiness that she did not want to be a part of. She went back to her car and drove, aimlessly at first, but gradually gravitating towards the one place and person that she thought she might be able to talk to. She sat in her car, in the same place she had parked a few days previously, looking at Chris's red front door and trying to decide how stupid she was being. Would he want to see her? What interest would he have in her domestic affairs? None, that was the answer to both questions. She called Polly's number, but it went straight to voicemail and left her sitting staring absently through the windscreen.

A sharp knock on the side window startled her from her reverie. She turned ready to apologise for parking in the wrong place or whatever it was she had done. Chris smiled in. She opened the window and tried to smile back.

"Are you looking for me?"

"No, yes, I mean not really. I think so yes."

"Well, you covered all the bases there."

"I mean yes, I was going to knock on your door, but I didn't want to disturb you if you were busy."

She could see now that Chris had his keys in his hand, she turned her head slightly and saw his car parked directly behind hers, he must have pulled up while she was busy looking in the wrong direction.

"Well, I was, but I'm not now. Come on in and I'll put the kettle on."

He straightened up and walked towards his house without looking back to see if she would follow, she hurriedly got out of the car and locked it. By the time she caught up he had opened the door, he stepped aside and invited her in with a wave of his hand.

"Come on in, sorry it's a bit of a mess, I've been trying to sort things out today."

"Don't worry about it, I'm sure it's fine."

There were some boxes and bin bags piled in the hallway, other than that it was clean and presentable. Chris followed her in and led her to the kitchen where, true to his word, he filled the kettle and got some mugs out. The furnishings and fittings were old, but not in a worn out or dilapidated way, the kitchen had a lived-in, loved feel to it. It felt homely in a way that a new kitchen never could.

"I'm really sorry to intrude like this, I know you must be really busy."

"Not at all, I've just about had enough for the day, I was just going to work out what I might have for tea. What can I do for you?"

"Well, actually I wanted to see if you're okay, it's been pretty hectic at work recently and I have seen you much. I just wondered if you were ok after, well, you know, after that thing with Kiera."

His face flickered into a grimace and his eyes rolled slightly, quickly resetting to the smile that he had been wearing previously;

"Oh my goodness, I've had worse than that. I just can't believe how ungrateful she was. Water under the bridge now, eh? How was work today?"

He poured some hot water into the pot, swilling it round and emptying it into the sink before putting in some tea bags and topping it up. He bought it to the table with two mugs and a carton of milk from the fridge.

"Oh, work was quiet. Lagrange is still keeping a low profile, thank goodness, it means we can all get on with our work."

Chris chuckled as he splashed some milk into the mugs and started pouring the tea.

"I know what you mean, I'm sure things would go smoother if he stayed home all the time."

He slid a blue mug of steaming tea across the table to Bev, which she gratefully took and cupped in her hands.

"You get the special visitor's mugs" he smiled, "I would've been in so much trouble if I ever gave Auntie Jean one with something funny written on it."

"I'm honoured then."

In truth, he had had no visitors since the funeral. He also suspected that the insistence on giving Auntie Jean the special mugs had not come from Jean herself, she was most interested in the biscuits. The thought jolted him;

"Would you like a biscuit?" he asked, starting to stand up and to get some from the cupboard.

"No, really I'm fine, it's nearly tea time."

"Well, if you're sure, I wouldn't want you telling everyone what a dreadful host I am."

They both smiled. Now Bev was here she was happy to have a friendly face across the table. She found she didn't want to talk about Dave after all, she actually wanted to talk about anything but. Chris didn't deserve to have to sit and listen to her complain about married life, she was sure he had enough on his plate already without having to listen to her trivial problems.

"How are things now?" she asked, gesturing vaguely around the room in what she hoped would be interpreted as a question about how things had been going since the funeral. It was.

"It's quiet, but it's okay. If I'm being honest, I'm kind of glad it's over. I still miss her though, keep expecting to go into a room and she'll be in there, waiting for me to fetch her a cup of tea or ask me about something or other."

"I know, it's hard, and I know what you mean. I kept expecting it to be my mum every time the phone rang for ages after she died. But I was glad she wasn't in pain anymore."

The memory made her tear up slightly, not full-blown crying, but moist eyes and a lump in her throat. She sipped her tea and then changed the subject;

"Tim's talking about his leaving do, he wants everybody to meet up somewhere for drinks. You'll be going along won't you?"

"I'm not sure, I don't feel very sociable right now. You know how it is?"

"Tim would be really disappointed if you didn't come, he specifically asked me to make sure you come."

"I could probably pop along, when is it?"

"He didn't say yet, and don't be such a misery, you know he thinks the world of you. He thinks he only got taken on because you told Jim Potter you would personally keep an eye on him."

This was actually true, but Chris hadn't realised that it was public knowledge. Tim had been his project, he had thought he'd seen some potential in him and had persuaded Jim to give him a chance in spite of his lack of qualifications and experience. Who was he to judge people for lack of exams? He had to work for all his after he had finished not going to school. He was glad he had been right, Tim had done well, and in truth Chris had only needed to keep an eye on him for the first six months, once he got something he got it.

"I suppose so, of course I'll go. I don't know if I'll last the course though, I'm unsteady enough on my feet without having one too many. Also, I don't want to start getting all maudlin and self-pitying."

He said it with a smile, but there was an element of truth in both of the statements.

"We'll go together, safety in numbers and all that. I'll make sure you don't fall over if you make sure I don't make a fool of myself after two drinks."

"It's a deal, won't Dave be coming along then?"

"I doubt it, we're not really speaking right now."

"Oh, I'm sorry to hear that, is everything okay?"

Now that the subject had come up Bev found she really didn't want to talk about Dave, she still needed time to process what she had found out, to try and make sense of it all. She didn't want to add to Chris's stress levels either, he'd had a hard enough time recently without having to listen to her woes and worries.

"I'm sure it'll be fine, we just need some time to sit down and sort it out."

"Well, let me know if there's anything I can do. Even if it's just coming round here and drinking tea while I witter."

"You don't witter, you're a good listener."

"What?"

"I said…. Oh, for goodness sake."

Chris smiled and stood up;

"Want to see how the garden's doing? It's been fabulous so far this year."

He led her to the back door and out into the late evening sun that glistened on the leaves, still shining and luminous after an earlier shower. The colours shone vibrantly and Chris and Bev walked through the damp grass and talked plants and flowers. Bev found it interesting and distracting in equal measures. Listening to Chris talk about the varieties and different things he had used to create his beautiful little garden made her think how wasted he was in the back office of GardenCo. She knew why he wanted to stay out of sight, but couldn't help thinking how his enthusiasm and obvious knowledge would be an asset to other parts of the centre.

Eventually, with tea drunk and the garden admired Bev felt she had imposed long enough. Chris strenuously denied that this was the case, but she didn't want to outstay her welcome and did want to get home and see if Dave had returned yet.

"Can I use the loo before I go? I don't want to get caught short on my way back."

"Sure, up the stairs and it's the door straight in front of you."

"Thanks."

Bev went upstairs, as she passed the open door of his bedroom she couldn't resist looking in. The neatness and tidiness of the room was admirable. She glanced at the computer on his well-ordered desk and saw that it was open on something called 'Mr Angree', she took it all in and moved on to the small room. When she was done she made her goodbyes with Chris and walked back to the car as he waved and went back inside.

CHAPTER 19

REORGANISING

The door closed and Chris stood for a moment in the hallway.

It had been nice to see Bev, unexpected but nice. He thought she had looked distracted and harried when he first saw her, sitting in her car gazing at her phone screen. She had chatted easily enough once the pot of tea was on the go. He wondered what had really led her to call round as he went back into the kitchen to make his own tea, maybe he would try and find out tomorrow at work, if they got a quiet moment.

He eschewed the TV in favour of listening to some music, not the old punk stuff tonight. Instead, he had opted for some of the music he had replaced it with in the 90's, when angry music had a resurgence. A compilation CD he had burned with Nirvana, Sonic Youth, Mudhoney and The Breeders all of whom vied for a place in his regular playlists. The energy and pace of the music galvanised him into getting up and continuing his work clearing away the now redundant clothes, artefacts and mementos that were placed around the house. He didn't throw out everything, some things held precious memories, a rarity from the times when he had not always been happy. Those were the good times that he wanted to hold on to and remember, like a talisman warding off the darker days.

The bags in the hallway continued to multiply and Chris resigned himself to spending another of his days off ferrying things away from the house. Still, looking around it was worth it. The house looked – different. It was no longer a shared space, but his own things took their new positions as if standing guard over his position as sole occupant. It was bittersweet, but he knew he had to do that to start to move on.

Unconsciously, he started talking under his breath, making a verbal list of what was done and what still needed doing. As he walked around muttering quietly to himself, he continued to adjust and rearrange things. The chair and sofa changed places, not without some additional grunting and expletives, then moved back when he realized he couldn't open the door properly. The bed was made up with clean linen, new sheets that they had been saving. He wasn't sure what it was they were saving them for, but this seemed as good a time as any. He took down the huge print of two horses standing outside a straw roofed farmhouse and leaned it against the wall, he would have to look for something to replace it, but no rush.

Finally, he sat down and took a deep breath. All the activity had been purposeful, or had felt it at the time. He now wondered what the purpose was, had he been keeping himself busy? Was he trying to remember, or trying to forget? He didn't know, only that it felt right, felt good. Absently he thought that he would need to explain all this, that he would be held to account. But the only person who was likely to object wasn't in a position to anymore. He stared at the blank TV screen, the music had ended a while back, he had been so preoccupied that he had barely noticed.

He sat beside the bed and talked. He talked about anything and everything, the minutiae and irrelevances of his day-to-day life;

"I saw Bill at the Post Office, he said to say hello. He's been to visit his daughter in Kent, you remember Tracey. He told me all about her, her children are all growing up he says. Not surprising really, he showed me a photo of them, insisted in fact. I only went in to get a stamp to post off that letter to the bank I was telling you about, I don't know why they can't have it online. Anyway, I was in there for nearly half an hour in the end."

He looked up and she nodded then gestured to the table by the bed with a small wave of her hand that wasn't wired up to the intravenous drip. He reached over and passed her the carton of

119

juice, holding the straw to her mouth as she took several sips. He placed it back down on the table and she gave him a small smile and a tired nod. He continued;

"There, that's better, I may go and get myself a cup of tea in a minute, not that the stuff from the machine is any good. It's just warm brown water really, still, it's better than nothing. I remembered to bring some change today."

He patted his pocket, making the aforementioned change jangle slightly,

"I see Aunty Jean's been in."

He nodded towards the grapes and reached over and helped himself to some, popping one into his mouth.

"She seems to have quite got the hang of the busses now, doesn't she? It's almost as if she enjoys it, I think she does really. I don't know that I'd want to get the bus everywhere, but then she doesn't have to get to work or anything does she? She's looking well on it too; I think it's given her a new lease of life."

He squeaked loudly as he adjusted himself on the uncomfortable vinyl chair and looked across at her pale, drawn face. She looked back at him, her eyes were still alert and alive, but they had lost the indefinable spark that had accompanied her lust for life. Most of what he could see now was the pain that had become a constant for her. The small shape under the bedclothes shifted and she nodded gently at him to show she had been listening.

"Work's mad at the moment, we got a big delivery in yesterday. All the staff have been flat out getting it onto the shelves and it's been selling as fast as we can get it out. It's the good stuff, from Simon's nursery. I've told you about him, haven't I? Used to work in the city and said he woke up one morning and realised he hated it so he sunk all his money into house with a couple of fields and put up a bunch of polytunnels. Never met a happier man!"

A nurse bustled in,

"I need to check how we're doing and do some meds; I won't be long."

She started to pull the curtain closed behind her and Chris took the hint.

"I'll go and get that cup of tea I promised myself, I'll see you in a bit."

He smiled and gave her a thumbs up which she acknowledged silently as the nurse started fussing around looking at charts, taking temperatures and checking the drip. The cup of tea was every bit as disgusting as he knew it would be, he sipped it as he stood by the vending machine watching the flow of people; purposeful doctors, orderlies pushing wheelchairs – empty and full, family members looking lost and people in dressing gowns in various stages of recovery. When he got back the nurse was finishing up.

"I've given her something for the pain, to make her more comfortable, she'll probably sleep now."

She probably would, that was it for the day now. He sat and finished his tea while he watched her sleep then gently covered her with her bedsheet and went home.

With one last look around the newly reorganised room Chris got up and collected his jacket from by the front door. He checked his wallet was in the pocket and that he had his keys then went out.

CHAPTER 20

EVEN BUSIER

The glass washer had been going just about non-stop all evening and Roger had already been down to the cellar twice, once to change a barrel and once to collect a fresh bottle of Jaeger and some more Red Bull, which he had started stocking at the request of his new customers. Another round of Jaeger Bombs was in the offing as the large group of young men and women continued to celebrate the birthday of one of their group. An increasing number of them had been arriving since mid-afternoon, taking selfies, talking loudly, laughing and getting steadily drunker as the day turned to evening. They had taken over most of the pub now, spilling out onto the pavement as they took turns to go out and smoke.

He was run off his feet, he had even called in Bethany for an extra pair of hands. She was glad of the extra shift, and the money that was coming into the till more than offset the extra he would have to pay her. It was a good day in The Crown, a few more days like this and he might be able to afford some of the improvements he had been putting off for a while. He smiled and started setting out some glasses as a woman in a leopard skin print dress came to the bar, cash card in hand, and he started filling the glasses.

The juke box had been turned up, at the request of the birthday boy, and a steady stream of coins were being deposited to ensure the ongoing cacophony of thumping bass and electronic beats. A couple of the girls had moved a table and were dancing in the middle of the floor. The few regulars that hadn't beaten a retreat were safely nestled at tables as far from the noisy crowd as they could get, although when they came to the bar the general consensus seemed to be that it was nice to see the place lively for a change.

Bethany looked over as Chris came in and smiled in greeting as she started pouring him a drink before he got to the bar. Roger was busy collecting empties and clearing tables with his back to the door. At first nobody else seemed to notice his arrival as he collected and paid for his pint which he took to an empty table near the door. Bethany turned back to the next customer and carried on serving.

The next person to come through the door was a returning smoker, a lad in tight jeans with ripped knees and a bright red Adidas shirt. He was talking loudly on his phone, swaying slightly and weaving back towards the group. His course took him past Chris's table which he nudged slightly with his hip, causing the freshly poured drink to splash slightly over the edge of the glass.

"Ah, sorry mate. Did you lose much of that? I can get you another."

"No problem, it was only a drop. I'm fine."

"Ok, cool."

He took his eyes away from his phone and looked at the offending puddle of beer and then up at Chris. His face gave away his immediate response to seeing the scarred and drooping eye, although he said nothing, just smiled drunkenly and carried on with his journey. He re-joined the group and retrieved his own drink, inserting himself back into a circle of friends and putting his arm around the waist of the woman in the leopard print dress. He listened to what was being talked about briefly, before turning and speaking into her ear, then nodding his head back in the direction of the door. Now leopard skin dress woman also looked in Chris's direction, staring for longer than was polite or necessary before turning back and whispering something back to Red shirt man then saying something to the group. Before long a ripple had passed among the party and most, if not all, of them had a not so surreptitious look in his direction. Some had stared, some sniggered and some could not help but let a look of revulsion wash across their faces.

Roger refilled the glass washer and looked over at Bethany who was busy pouring out some glasses of the nondescript white wine that they made such a healthy profit from. He smiled at her and then was distracted by a flash from the group of revellers. More selfies? How many pictures could you take of yourself before it got stale. Only it wasn't, this time the flash had been directed across the room. He looked and saw that several phones were pointed towards Chris, he hadn't even noticed him when he'd arrived and now saw him looking awkward and uncomfortable.

"Oi, smile." A voice shouted.

"Come on, wave for us." Called another.

There were several more flashes, then another voice rose above the music;

"Hey, Quasimodo, where's Esmerelda?"

Chris's expression changed from irritated to angry. Roger felt angry too, he came around the bar and stood in front of the phone wielding group.

"All right, that's enough, leave the other customers alone."

There were some sniggers, someone at the back muttered;

"Get out of the way grandad."

"Enough, or the party's over okay."

"Yeah, whatever."

"All right, keep your hair on."

The group settled and carried on talking to each other, went back to their drinks with occasional, inaudible, comments clearly aimed at him and laughter. He turned back to where Chris was sitting, to check he was okay. But it was empty now, only a three quarters full pint glass sitting in a small rivulet of beer that was slowly making its way to the edge of the table. He picked up his cloth from the bar and went to clean it up. He would have to make it up to Chris next time he came in, apologise and give him one on the house, it seemed like the least he could do. He walked back over to the rowdy group and collected up some more empty glasses as they danced, laughed and shouted.

CHAPTER 21

AWOL

T he house was still empty. The silence made the jangle sound loud as she put her keys in the bowl by the front door, her footsteps seemed to echo on the laminated hall floor as she went in. Nobody had been in the kitchen; everything was still exactly as she had left it. She checked Dave's office, the splintered drawer still lay half way open, nothing else seemed to have been moved. She went back to the kitchen and made herself a cup of coffee and a sandwich which she sat and ate in front of the TV, a programme about a couple bankrupting themselves with an over ambitious house building project involving cranes, girders, unfeasibly large windows and inconceivably large amounts of money. Good luck to them, Bev switched off the TV and went upstairs, where she found the first signs that anybody had been in the house.

In the bedroom the wardrobe door was left wide open, the space where Dave's suits and shirts would normally be hanging was mostly empty. His drawers were similarly left half open and half empty and the suitcase which usually rested on top of the wardrobe was missing. Bev stood in the room looking around, then looked back in the wardrobe and drawers to check again, as if she might have somehow been mistaken or that something may have changed since she last looked.

Bewildered, she got out her phone and checked for missed calls, nothing. Next, she tried calling Dave. His phone went straight to voicemail, she left a short message asking him to ring back. Not knowing what to do next she lay down on the bed and cried, sobbing silently into the pillow without knowing if it was anger or relief that was causing it.

She awoke later, it was now dark outside and the room felt cold and lifeless. She went back downstairs to make more coffee and check her phone again, then sat an composed a long text that she deleted before she pressed send. She was angry with Dave for all the deception and lies, she didn't know what to do next or how to fix this, and she still had no idea why he had spent that £200 at a jeweller's shop. But they had been married for a long time, long enough for her to know his habits and routines, what made him laugh, what food he liked and how he liked his tea. At least, she thought she did. Now she didn't know where he was or what he was doing or why he had taken his things and she was scared. She tried calling Polly again, but her phone was still off.

She went into Dave's office and started to look through any paperwork she could find, in the hope that it might offer some kind of clue as to where he was or what his secret other life might consist of. She had decided that if she needed to break into any more locked drawers she would, and had taken the big screwdriver in with her. In the event it was not necessary, everything was open and accessible She was disappointed that the first pieces of paper she looked at did not offer up any illuminating clues or evidence, like it did on the TV shows she liked to watch – 'aha! An important piece of information on the second page of the book I just picked up!' However, she persevered, looking through diaries, notebooks and old receipts assiduously while she sipped her coffee.

By 1 o'clock in the morning she had found only two things that interested her; in amongst the general miasma of clutter and junk there had been an address book. It was clearly old and did not contain many contacts, those that were there where mostly landline numbers next to forenames, a mixture of male and female names. She had put that to one side and then found a notebook. When she started to flick through, she could see it just contained bullet pointed lists of things Dave needed to do and things he needed to remember. Most of these went back years and the book had been abandoned about a third of the way in. She nearly threw it back into the drawer, but on a whim, she turned to the back of the book and looked at the final page. It was a neatly printed list of all his various online places and spaces, next to each one was written his password for that account. Bev didn't know if they were all up to date, but the fact that some had been crossed out and amended made her think they probably were. She put the book on the desk next to the Dave's computer and switched on.

She had now resigned herself to a late night. In the kitchen she made a strong (two spoons) cup of coffee which she took back into the office, cradling it in her hands and enjoying the smell and the warmth of it. She set it down on the coaster next to the keyboard and folded the notebook open. Running her finger down the list she tried to decide where to start, where she might begin to find the real Dave. In the end indecisiveness ruled the day, she opted instead to simply work her way down the list and see what she could find.

By the time her cup only contained half an inch of cold coffee she had covered the first four of his places on the list. One which the password had expired, two others that had very little activity over the last couple of years, according to their welcome screens Dave had not logged into either of them for over a year. The fourth had turned out to be a very dull chat group that Dave had used to talk to people about golf. Just reading the posts had nearly been enough to send her off into her much-needed sleep. She yawned and stretched, it was gone two now, but in or a penny in for a pound.

After a trip to the loo – all that coffee had to go somewhere, she refilled her mug and settled back down to her task. She was so tired now that she was not even sure what she was looking for any more. What clues was she expecting to find? Where Dave might be? Why he was so angry with her and Polly? What he was up to when he wasn't at home? She really didn't know; all she knew for sure was that she had to try and make sense of what was happening.

Her eyes started to have trouble focussing as she clicked and scrolled her way through unfamiliar websites, she became more aimless in her search and was at the point of admitting defeat, giving up and going to bed. Currently she was on the members page of the bloody golf clubs boring bloody website, she was looking at pages and pages of photos from club days, social events, Stableford competitions, Captain's day - along with regular days on the green and people celebrating particularly good scores. She really didn't get it; she had tried to show an interest but could find no charm in the game. Dave appeared occasionally in pictures, smiling at the camera. Although infrequent it was still more often than she would have expected for someone who only played once a week. She didn't linger any longer than she needed to on his familiar face, she was ready to turn in now, the golf club had finished her off. She came to the bottom of another page and paused. There was something though, it had snagged her subconscious and lodged there, something that was so subliminal that she had no inkling what it was. She went back through the same page, pausing and looking carefully at Dave's image when it appeared. Still nothing.

Finally, she gave up for the night. She put her now empty cup in the sink and checked the doors were locked, it didn't look as if anybody else was coming home tonight. She went upstairs where the red light of the clock told her it was 2.45. Shit, she was too tired now to even undress, she lay on the bed and pulled the half of the duvet she wasn't lying on over, wrapping herself in a cocoon. Now though, her mind was racing. In spite of her fatigue and the lateness of the hour, she lay awake knowing that she would never be able to get to sleep.

She snapped awake at 5.30, wide awake. The clock was the only light in the room, everywhere else it was still dark and the silence was complete. There were no birds welcoming in the day yet, it was too early for traffic and none of the hubbub of the day which orientates us during the waking hours was present.

In this drifting island of darkness Bev lay curled in the warmth of the duvet, her mouth tasted of coffee and she badly needed to pee again. She tried to fight it and go back to sleep, but her bladder wouldn't let her, she stumbled out of bed and was sitting on the loo when it hit her. She realized what it was that had been staring her in the face all the time.

Hurriedly pulling up her underwear and trousers, wide awake again now, she went back downstairs. She woke the computer back up, it was still on the same dull golf club page she had left it on, and started to scroll through the photos again. She was right, her mind had used her brain's downtime to decode and decipher what she had seen, and now she could not unsee it, but she had no idea what it meant.

In every picture of Dave there was another man either next to or near him. It was not one of Dave's usual friends; Bev knew them all, they'd been to their house, she'd met their wives and been out with them and their various partners on rare occasions. This was nobody she recognised; his side parted silver hair groomed in keeping with his smart attire which bordered on dapper. In two of the pictures he had his arm casually draped across Dave's shoulders in a chummy 'lads together' kind of way.

Refuelling herself with yet more coffee she sat and looked at the pictures trying to work out what it was she found disquieting. She read the man's name in one of the captions, it was not a name she was familiar with, it had no resonance, rang no bells. A Google search only led her back to the same golf club photos, Bev sat and stared at the monitor as the breaking dawn started to light the room, chasing away the shadows, waking the birds and chasing away the silence of the night.

CHAPTER 22

KNACKERED – AND YOU?

Their two cars pulled into the staff parking area simultaneously. Chris and Bev walked inside together, crunching across the car park and into the staff entrance.

"Morning Chris, how are you?"

"Knackered, not enough sleep. You?"

"Same, I hope Lagrange leaves us alone today."

"Yeah, fat chance, what kept you awake?"

"Oh, you know, old bones mostly. You?"

"I think my head was working overtime, too much going on."

Each knew that the other was not telling the whole truth, and each was too tired to try and find out what was up. In truth, they both looked haggard and tired. Bev hadn't been back to bed after her early morning start, instead she had showered, put on fresh clothes and gone for a walk while she tried to make sense of things.

Chris had got home earlier than he had planned after the confrontation with the party goers. The shame, embarrassment and anger burning in him as he clenched and unclenched his fists and bit the inside of his lip. In his imagination he had marched back into the pub and delivered brutal justice to the people who'd laughed, pointed and taken photos. In reality he got home, fumbled for his keys and let himself in with a noise that was half sigh, half growl.

131

In the hallway Poquelin was waiting. He stood, legs splayed, one hand on his hip the other resting on top of a Poquelin sized baseball bat. He shook his head slowly from side to side, tutting his tongue, then lifted the bat and pointed it at Chris.

"You really need to show them. You need to give them some hell. Bastards, who the bloody hell do they think they are?" He turned and stomped into the kitchen, kicking one of the chairs as he passed it. Chris followed, catching the chair and resetting it as it teetered on the verge of falling.

"How bloody dare they?" He swept his arm across the draining board, knocking two mugs onto the floor. One skidded and skittered under the table, the other landed with a dull cracking sound as the handle became detached and the mug split don the middle.

"Okay, I get it, let's not smash all the mugs though."

Poquelin was not listening, he flapped his ridiculous, improbable wings and half-jumped onto the counter where he opened the cupboard over the microwave. This was where the emergency whiskey was kept. There had been a lack of emergencies recently, so the bottle he pulled out was three quarters full. Tucking his bat under his arm he twisted off the cap and took several large gulps then passed it to Chris. He took it and filled his own mouth with the sweet burning liquid, feeling it sear its way down his throat. He shook his head slightly and grimaced, whiskey was not really his drink of choice. In spite of this he took another large gulp as Poquelin spread his wings and glided clumsily back down to floor level. He strode past Chris and into the sitting room muttering to himself;

"Bastards, bastards, bastards, bastards, bastards."

Chris followed with the whiskey and arrived to see Poquelin swing his bat onto the cushions on the sofa, sending up a little puff of dust. He repeated this with the other cushions, muted 'whumps' punctuated by mutters of 'bastards' over and over. He took the bottle back and had another swig then tossed it back to Chris who barely managed to not drop it.

"Bastards, bastards, bastards." Now he kicked out at the painting of the horses which was still leaning against the wall. There was a loud cracking noise and the frame broke, leaving the picture itself dangling from the unbroken side and the horses standing on a perilously steep slope.

"Stop smashing things up!"

"Why? Why should I? I'm so fucking angry, they're bastards." He picked up the cushion closest to him and threw it across the room, where it knocked the clock off the mantlepiece. The cushion landed on the floor and the clock tumbled on top of it, landing softly. Chris bent to pick it up and turned it over in his hand to check it was okay.

"I said, stop smashing things."

The request went unheard, Poquelin had already left the room. Chris heard him skitter up the stairs, followed by a series of bumps and crashes.

"No! Not my records again!! Pack it in."

He followed upstairs and found Poquelin in the other room, not his. He was tipping things over, kicking them and then hitting them with his bat; the chair, the stool, an empty box. Chris went into the room and he stopped, turned and looked at him;

"Come on, aren't you angry? You should be. Help me smash this stuff."

"How is that going to help?"

"It'll get it all out of your system, you'll feel better."

"What, if the house is trashed I'll feel better?"

"Well yeah," Poquelin paused, "It's more about the process really, best not to overthink these things."

"No, stop breaking things. Please, just stop,"

He realised he was still holding the bottle and took another mouthful of whiskey then held the bottle out. As Poquelin took it Chris deftly plucked the baseball bat from his other hand,

"That's enough."

"No, it's never enough. You need to do something about it, you need to sort this out. Every time you let them get away with this it makes you a bit smaller. Sort it out."

"Sort it out? It'll never be sorted out. Don't you get it? This has been my whole life, being stared at, laughed at, put down, cut off. It's not going to end, ever."

Chris sat heavily on the bed and put his head in his hands. The room was silent except for the sound of his breathing as he wiped tears away with his palms. He had expected the bashing and crashing to continue, when it didn't he tentatively drew his hands away from his face. Poquelin was standing silently in the middle of the floor gazing at him with his ruby eyes.

"What?"

"I never took you for a quitter."

"No? Well I am, I'm tired of being the butt of everybody's joke, I'm tired of fighting it, I'm just tired."

He slumped and looked dejectedly at Poquelin, who in turn put his fists to either side of his face and twisted them;

"Boo hoo, break out the violins. You poor thing, why don't you try having wings, scales and claws and being 2 foot tall, then you'd know what it was like to be pointed at and outcast. There are other people worse off than you you know?"

"Fuck off, go fuck yourself you little twat."

"Ooh, there you go, that's fighting talk now, that's what I'm talking about. I'm a little offended by the sizeist comments, but at least you've stopped whinging. Listen, it's simple, you need to strike first, get in the first hit, show them you're bossing it. Also you need to help me smash the house up of course, that's the main thing right now."

"Do not smash the house up."

Chris climbed fully into bed and pulled the duvet over himself with his back turned to Poquelin. The house remained quiet and he fell into a deep and troubled sleep.

Waking up the next morning was easy, it was the opening his eyes and actually moving that was hard. He managed it by increments, one eye, one arm, one leg, until eventually all parts of him were able to move cautiously around the house, going from room to room and surveying the damage. There was a lot of surface mess; things tipped over, scuff marks on walls and doors, pillows scattered around. He found the whiskey where he had left it, with only a finger of liquid left in the bottom of the bottle.

Downstairs was also not badly hurt, with the exception being the broken mugs in the kitchen which he carefully swept up and dropped in the bin. The painting looked sad dangling lopsidedly in its broken frame, seeing it like this made him realise how attached to it he actually was, it had been her favourite. He decided it had won a reprieve from the charity shop, he would get it reframed and put it back in its rightful place. The thought cheered him slightly, he took some painkillers for his aching head and started setting the house to rights before putting on his GardenCo fleece and leaving the house.

CHAPTER 23

WHAT'S UP?

C hris slogged his way through the foothills of his morning until he reached a point where his body was clamouring for some caffeine and his head was quietly asking for some more painkillers, to try and shift the ache that started behind his eyes and travelled through his skull to his neck and shoulders. He found a box of paracetamol crushed at the back of his desk drawer and slipped it into his pocket leaving his hands free to carry his empty mug to the staffroom. The smell of the coffee as he brewed it started to have its own mystical effect that he hoped the tablets would add the finishing touches to.

"Need some wake up juice eh? Put some in here please."

Bev put her own mug on the worktop next to Chris's, he spooned in a heap of coffee powder and added steaming water. He passed it to Bev who had sat at the table;

"No offence Chris, but you look like shit. Are you okay?"

"Nothing a coffee and these won't fix." He took the box from his pocket, sat across from Bev and prised two small white pills from their plastic houses.

"No offence to you either, but you don't look so great yourself."

"We'll call it quits then eh?" She cupped her mug with both hands and inhaled the steam. "What's up?"

"I decided to enjoy some whiskey after you left, I'm just not enjoying it quite so much right now." He omitted to mention his aborted trip to the pub, not wanting to relive the humiliation in any way shape or form. "What about you?"

"Me and Dave argued, it was a late night."

Bev was now also guilty of the sin of omission, she too had her reasons, mostly that she didn't understand what was going on and didn't know what she was supposed to do next. Both suspected that the other had not told quite the whole story, but both maintained the status quo by not asking any more questions. Bev pointed at the notice board where an A4 poster had been pinned up on top of Lagrange's latest edict.

"Tim's leaving do, are you still going?"

The sign was painstakingly hand written, inviting everyone to join him at the Red Lion the following week. The Lion was the go-to pub for Potters staff to meet for celebrations, commiserations and general festivities, Tim had booked the function room. Chris could see him sitting at his kitchen table carefully printing the sign, getting Deborah to check his spelling as he went along, with several discarded attempts scrunched up on one side of the table and a look of concentration on his face. The finished poster was a work of art, including a very competent drawing of a champagne bottle firing it's cork up one side of the paper. The thought of going to a pub made his chest tighten, he sipped his coffee, testing the temperature before judging it to be okay to wash down his tablets.

"I don't know, probably, you?"

"I want to, but I hate going to things like that on my own."

"Won't Dave come with you?"

Bev's face crumpled slightly and Chris kicked himself as the look of hurt flashed across her face.

"He'll be out that night, he's already got something on."

Chris knew a hastily composed lie when he heard one – he should. He also knew when to stop asking questions, how bad could Tim's do be? It would be all people from work who knew him, had seen him often enough to have had their fill of staring surreptitiously at his wounded face.

"Why don't we go together? I'll chaperone you, and we can share a cab."

"Chaperone me? I'm not sure Tim's leaving do is going to be that sort of event, is it? Besides, there's not much danger of anybody chatting me up."

Chris thought there probably was actually, nevertheless he laughed with Bev.

"Me neither eh? We'll go together and be the undatables."

"Okay, that sounds like a not-date to me, let's do that."

It felt good that they had laughed, important somehow, they both took their coffee with them and went back to their respective work areas with tired smiles and the disquieting feeling that all was not well with the other, but no idea how to broach the subject.

CHAPTER 24

I CAN DO THAT

In spite of his tiredness and lingering headache Chris took a detour to a row of small shops near his house at the end of the day. The end shop was a picture framing business, windows filled with beautifully framed (what else would you expect?) paintings and art work by local artists alongside reproduction film posters and photos. He carefully lifted the picture from the back of his car and nursed it inside, holding the broken and jagged edges of the frame together with one hand.

"You just caught me, I was about to shut up."

"I'm glad I did, would you be able to do anything about this? See if it's fixable or put a new frame on it."

"I can certainly look, bring it around the back."

The man ran one hand across his closely cut scalp and gesticulated towards a door behind the counter leading to a brightly lit back room.

Chris followed him past frame samples comprising multiple multi-coloured chevrons, making their own work of right-angled art. He carefully set the picture down on a space on the framing table that was not covered with the tools and implements of the framing trade.

"Looks nice." The man glanced at the painting then up at the clock, "I'll have a look tomorrow, it looks salvageable but I won't know till

I've had a proper check, It's always best if you can keep something in its proper frame I think."

They had walked back to the counter where he passed Chris a slip of paper with a space for his name and phone number. Chris added his details and the man wrote 'Horses by stable' underneath then tore off a strip with a serial number printed on and gave it Chris.

"Thanks a lot, it's not beautiful, but it's been in the house for as long as I can remember."

"Did it get knocked down?"

"Yeah, something like that." Chris was sure he was unable to keep the embarrassment from his face, if not an actual blush. He turned towards the door.

"You'll give me a call then?"

"Yeah, later in the week, have a good one."

"You too, thanks."

CHAPTER 25

THINGS TO NOT DO

Again, the house was deserted and dark. Bev switched on the downstairs lights in an attempt to chase away the emptiness and started unpacking the shopping. She hadn't known whether to buy enough for one, two or three people, in the end she had compromised and got enough for two, but with enough extras to stretch it to three if necessary. Right now there did not seem to be any need for all of this food, there was still no reply from Dave and Polly had not reappeared since her last laundry visit.

She looked at the phone sitting hopefully on the counter. She had tried repeatedly to call Dave and was now starting to get annoyed that his phone kept going to voicemail, she was both angered by his lack of response, and also worried about his whereabouts. She wanted to tell Polly, but was scared of how she might react. Would she be heartbroken at Bev for misplacing Dave? Or would she treat her with the contempt she deserved for not being able to keep track of him? She had always been Dave's little princess after all. Besides, she would be out celebrating tonight, having handed in her last piece of coursework. Bev had texted her earlier and got a 'smiley face', 'thumbs up', 'kiss' in reply, but no actual words.

Now the food was all in its rightful places Bev had the sinking feeling that she didn't actually get anything that she liked, only a selection of Dave and Polly's favourite meals. Beans on toast it was then, the comfort of familiar childhood staples tasted good, sitting at the table by herself then deciding to leave the washing up – fuck it –

and run a hot, deep bath before having an early night. She tried
calling Polly and Dave again while the bath was running. Predictably
Dave's phone went straight to voicemail, a perfunctory message
asking her to leave her name and number, she declined. Polly's
phone rang several times, Bev was just about to ring off when
Polly's voice answered;

"Hi Mum." Her voice was loud, presumably to compensate for the
hubbub of music, talking and laughter in the background, the pub
then. "How are you? I'm at the pub."

"Hi Pol, all okay?"

"Yeah, all fine here, I'm at the pub."

"You said, well, have a good time, I'll speak to you...."

"What's that? I couldn't hear you, it's noisy here."

"I said I'll...."

"Sorry, I really can't hear you."

"Never mind, you have a nice night."

This last was almost shouted.

"Okay, I'll speak to you tomorrow."

A man's voice cut across whatever Polly said next.

"Bye then."

"Bye."

The call ended abruptly and Bev undressed. She looked at herself
in the mirror and decided she could maybe afford to skip a meal or
two, but not too bad at all - for her age. Then she sank into a tub full
of hot water and bubbles, for as long as she wanted, with nobody
needing to come in and 'just quickly use the loo.'

Relaxed now, Bev lay in bed and tried to sleep. She should have
been exhausted after the minimal amount of sleep she had last night,
but her brain wouldn't let her end the day yet, it kept sending
random thoughts chasing around her head, re-running conversations,

trying to guess or second guess where Dave might be. She resolved that if she didn't hear from him tomorrow, she would start ringing round his friends, and if that didn't work, she would call his work. If she still had no luck she would camp outside his office and wait for him.

These resolutions did not help her find peace, or sleep. If anything, they just sent more thoughts and questions running around her mind. She relocated to the comfy end of the sofa, with a furry blanket piled on top of herself, and flicked through the TV channels in a vain attempt to find something distracting. Everything was bright and multi-coloured and presented by teenagers, or factual and informative, presented by people in suits. She left the sanctuary of the sofa and moved to the computer, keeping the blanket draped around her shoulders. Here she flicked through websites in the same listless and aimless way she had been watching the TV.

She disappeared down a rabbit-hole of linked articles, videos and advertisements, clicking from one to another every 45 seconds or so with no genuine interest or enthusiasm. Most sites were clicked away before she had even finished reading the main heading.

At last she started to tire, her eyes were getting gritty and her weariness rushed up on her like an express train. She was searching for the website she had seen on Chris's computer, Mr Angree, as the page opened a huge yawn overtook her entire body, starting with a lungful of noisily inhaled breath that led to a tensing and relaxing of all her muscles and the surrender of her now watering eyes. She left the computer as it was and retreated to the sanctuary of her bed.

Her phone rang and she started awake, opening her eyes, snatching it up and sliding the green circle upwards.

"Morning Mum."

"Eh? Morning. What time is it?"

"Sorry, it's a bit early, I just wanted to catch you before you left for work."

"Oh, no problem. How was your evening?"

"It was okay, we didn't stay out too late, it was noisy and I was tired."

"I thought you'd be out celebrating 'till the wee small hours."

"No, save that for after the exams, then it'll be time for big partying. It's good to get that last assignment out of the way though."

"I bet, what are you up to today?"

"Revision timetable officially starts today, I'm already nervous. It's going to be no time before the exams."

"Yes, then they'll be over. You'll do fine love, you're clever and you work hard. I'm so proud of you."

"Thanks, how are you anyway?"

"Oh, I'm fine. Not sleeping too well at the moment."

"But you're okay?"

"Yes, yes, fine."

"Good, how about Dad?"

"He's, um, he's ah, fine – yes, he's fine."

"You don't sound so sure."

"No, I am, he's okay."

"Okay. Did you talk to him about the trip?"

Bev left a silence that hung for a couple of heartbeats too long.

"Are you okay, did I say something wrong?"

"No, no, not at all. Polly, can you come over this evening, after I've finished work?"

"Why, what's happened, what's wrong?"

"Nothing, I'll explain this evening."

"But you and Dad are both okay?"

"Yes."

144

"I'm sorry I didn't return your call sooner; I've been tied up with uni work."

"You don't need to apologise; I'll see you later okay. Do you want me to cook?"

"That would be nice, but why don't you wait for me to get there and we'll cook together? I'll bring some cakes for pudding."

"Ok, that sounds great. Half six then?"

"And you're sure you're okay?"

"Yes, revise. I'll see you later, I've got to get ready for work now."

"Love you."

"Love you too, see you later."

CHAPTER 26

HEART TO HEART

The following week was a quiet one for Chris, he stayed warily away from the pub, kept busy at work and made some choices about what colour paint to start giving the various rooms in the house. He wasn't convinced he'd made good choices, but as nobody else would see it he didn't much care. Besides, it was mostly variations on Magnolia anyway, no point going mad was there?

Once the paint started being applied he became lost in the task, enjoying the routine of the process and the calmness of the repetition as he methodically edged, rolled, undercoated, overcoated and glossed. It filled his evenings, accompanied by the sound of loud and unflinching music – punctuated at intervals by an unexpected introspective ballad or love song, thanks to the magic of random play. Well, we all have our guilty pleasures, Chris's was Dire Straits.

The sitting room was first on the list, crisp and clean, still smelling of paint, it was now definitely his own space. There was a place on the wall, waiting for the return of the horses once they had been repaired. The bedroom required less effort, being mostly comprised of four plain walls. Chris mused that he should maybe start calling it the spare room now, with a hint of sadness. He had now moved on to the kitchen which required some minor repairs, a good scrub and plenty of paint.

Poquelin had not shown his ugly face during this time, meaning Chris had not missed out on as much sleep as he had been recently. Tired from decorating in the evenings he had been tumbling into bed, leaving no time for writing his blog or mining the internet for nuggets of information, truths, half-truths and outright lies. Only a casual glance at his blog figures and an occasional scroll through the adverts and inanities of Facebook and Reddit.

The kitchen offered enough distraction for several evenings, and required more than one trip to the DIY store, but once it was done and Chris stood back to admire his handiwork he was transported back to a time when it had all been gleaming and new. A time before this house got tired, when it had been scrubbed to within an inch of its life and had been the safest, most welcoming place in a world where he did not always feel welcome.

His paint-spattered tee-shirt and jeans were now rolled up and put in the shed with the rest of the decorating paraphernalia, ready for next time, whenever that might be. Now his thoughts turned to Tim's leaving do. People at work were looking forward to it, passing on their way to their respective jobs and asking:

"What are you wearing?"

Meeting in the staffroom;

"Shall we get pizza first?"

Helping one another with larger jobs;

"What time shall we meet?"

Beyond agreeing to go with Bev he had made no plans or preparations for the evening at all, he had barely seen Bev and had not given himself time to think too much. When he did see her, she appeared distracted and distant, he caught up with her in the staff kitchen;

"Hi, are we still on for tomorrow?"

"Hi, oh yeah, what time shall I call by?"

"Eightish would be fine, are you okay?"

"Yeah, a bit of a week that's all."

"Anything I can do?"

No, thanks Chris, just be good company tomorrow. I really need cheering up."

"Good company is my middle name. Say if you need anything else though, won't you?"

"I will, thanks. Better get back before Lagrange goes and messes everything up."

"I know what you mean, see you tomorrow."

They both smiled and walked back towards their respective work areas, Bev with her own drink and another in a brightly coloured mug with a picture of a unicorn printed on the side – presumably for Kiera, who was now trusted to be left alone for periods of time; she was proving to be a fast learner and proficient worker. Some days Bev had been despatching her to different parts of the centre, to give her an idea of who everybody was and what they did; much as she had done when she had first started. She seemed to enjoy these trips away from reception, and had been well received by other members of the staff team. If only, thought Bev, she had some way of cutting the frostiness between Kiera and Chris.

She settled back on her chair and passed Kiera her mug, what had she just said to Chris? 'It's been a bit of a week', you could say that again, but this time add a few expletives of your choice and insert them randomly between the words to act as makeshift adjectives and superlatives. Even then that would not suffice to describe her week.

Polly had arrived early, as Bev had known she would. Her hair was flattened onto her scalp and the front of her university sweatshirt was damp where she had left her coat open and flapping as she walked. Bev hugged her as she came in then helped her peel off her jacket which they left dripping in the hallway as Bev passed her the kitchen towel to dry off her hair.

"What's up mum?" Polly asked as she passed over a carrier bag that she had been holding under her coat, the promised cakes. Bev already knew what the bag would contain – Bakewell tarts. The good thick soft ones from the baker on the corner of the local shops, these had been both their favourites for as long as she could remember. She turned away from Polly to put the kettle on, she didn't know what to say or how to say it now that Polly was here, where to start or how to make sense of anything. Polly started for her;

"Is it about the money? Did Dad have a paddy?"

"Well, kind of, you could say that." She put the teabags in the mugs and got the milk out of the fridge.

"It's okay, I kind of figured he would. But it was lovely of you to offer, I'm going to save like mad through the summer then hopefully I can get enough together to go later in the year, or maybe next year."

"Oh love, I've got some money I saved from my own pay. I want you to have it, I want you to go and have a good time, see the world, enjoy being young."

She couldn't help letting a tear run down her cheek as her voice cracked slightly. She was adding the final touches to the tea, Polly came up behind her and put her arms around her in a loose hug.

"What is it Mum? What's wrong?"

"Have you spoken to Dad this week?"

"No, he hardly ever rings me, you know how he is."

"You don't know where he is then?"

"Well, no, he's here isn't he? Or at work still?"

Bev sat down at the table and Polly joined her, they both blew on their tea and took a tentative sip. Feeling more composed now Bev gave Polly a potted rundown of the week's events, missing out some details that she didn't want to share yet. For her part Polly listened without interrupting, her expression changed from surprised to shocked, to angry as events unfolded.

"So you don't know where he is either then?"

149

"No, no idea."

"I'm not surprised about the money, he's always been tight It's what he does to you. I'll call him."

She sat the phone on the table between them where they both heard it ring, then go to his familiar, impersonal, voicemail message.

"Dad, it's Polly, can you give me a call when you get this message?" she looked up, "Where do you think he might be?"

"I've no idea. I've tried his work but he's taken leave 'for personal reasons.' I've tried calling his friends but they either don't know or won't say. I don't know what to do next."

"Have you called the police?"

"Apparently, if he's booked leave and packed a suitcase, they assume he's gone on holiday, or so I was informed by the patronising lady when I called 911. Anyway, what did you mean just now?"

"When?"

"When you said 'it's what he does to you'."

"You know, the way he stops you doing things because they're too expensive, or the way he checks the receipts after you've done the weekly shop."

"That's just watching the money though, it's being careful."

"No Mum, it's the way he puts you down, the condescending way he talks to you and belittles you."

"He doesn't – does he?"

"All the time."

"What times?"

"Oh, come on, you know when you got your job and he tried to talk you out of it, told you you'd be stupid to do it? Or when he just barely gives you enough money for the shopping and you have to put things back at the checkout."

"You can't remember that, and he didn't say I was too stupid, he said it would be too difficult for me."

"I do remember, and it's the same thing. Can't you see how he's been bossing you around and putting you down for years? When did you last go out for a drink with your friends or out for a meal? Why do you think I stay out so much? I can't stand it when he treats you like that, and he was starting to do it to me too."

There was silence. Bev sat and picked her thumbnail as she recalled painfully the times Dave had belittled her, memory after memory. But that couldn't be right, he loved her, they were married, they had a daughter together. She stared at the table then looked up at Polly. Polly's face had a strange mixture of kindness, empathy and fear fighting for dominance, her eyes brimmed as she spoke;

"Sorry Mum, I'm sorry. I know you can't see it, but I can. He's been like it all my life, it's only spending time at Fred's house and seeing how his parents are that made me realise what it is. It's abuse Mum."

Another long silence as Bev stared back at the table, then in a small voice;

"What can I do?"

"No Mum," Polly came round the table and put her arms around Bev, "Not you – us. We're in this together, you're not on your own."

"Okay, what can we do?"

"Well, first things first, we've got Bakewells, I think better after cake. Secondly I think we need something more substantial than this."

She took the cups of cold tea and put them by the sink then rummaged in the cupboard, emerging with a half-empty bottle of Pernod.

"Christ, is this really all you've got? Never mind, it'll have to do.

CHAPTER 27

AT THE PARTY

The party was in full swing, Tim was happily intoxicated and moving around the room hugging everyone, thanking them for coming, telling them how much he'd miss them and accepting offers of drinks. Deb, charming and smiling as always was at his side. When Chris and Bev had arrived, Tim made a beeline to them. "I'm so glad you're here, I've hardly seen you this week, what can I get you to drink?"

"I wouldn't have missed it for the world, you know that, and put your wallet away, I'm getting these. Hi Deb, how are you doing? You're looking great."

Chris smiled and couldn't help himself from briefly looking down at the sequined top stretched tightly across her abdomen.

"You too Chris." She caught his glance and smiled conspiratorially, "I knew he'd tell you, how are you though? How are you managing?"

Chris still didn't know how to respond when people asked him how he was doing after the funeral, but Deb put him at ease, something in the way she asked the question; matter-of-factly with real concern but no expectation of a response.

"Thanks, and congratulations to you. What are you drinking?"

"Diet Coke, of course. Come on I'll help you carry them."

She linked her arm in his and walked to the bar with him, where he ordered a round of drinks. Tim and Bev re-joined them just as Chris was paying.

"Well, to Tim in his newest adventures." The four of them raised their glasses and took a drink, smiling conspiratorially over the shared secret of what Tim's other new adventure was - besides changing jobs. It was clear that Tim had told Bev now and she beelined to Deb, steering her away and practically interrogating her about every detail from scans to dates to details of how Deb was feeling. The beam on Deb's face gave the answer to that away immediately.

Tim stayed next to Chris, presumably happy for a bit of non-baby related conversation.

"How's things? You've been low-profile recently, not avoiding me now I've defected are you?"

"No, nothing like that, I've been trying to sort the house out, get rid of things I don't need and tidy the place up."

"Ah, sorry mate, that must be hard eh? You will give me a shout if there's anything you need a hand with, won't you?"

"Yeah thanks, some things you just need to do yourself really. You know how it is?"

"I guess so, the offer still stands though, shout out if I can help with anything."

"I will, thanks. Debs is looking well, how is she?"

"A bit of morning sickness, mostly in the evening. I don't know why they call it that really. Still, it means we always have plenty of biscuits in the house right now."

"Biscuits?"

"Yeah, apparently they help with morning sickness, especially ginger nuts. Who knew eh?"

"Not me, but nothing much surprises me nowadays. You all set for the new job?"

"Can't wait to start if I'm being honest, I've had enough of Mr Knownothing telling me how I should be doing my job."

"I know exactly what you mean, and speak of the devil…."

They both looked over to the door where Lagrange had just walked in, he was looking around the room scanning the faces of the other attendees. His suit would have been suitable for a wedding, complete with a matching tie and pocket handkerchief.

"Did you invite him?"

"I didn't not invite him, it was just a general invite wasn't it? It was only on the staffroom board, I didn't think he ever went in there. I certainly didn't expect to see him here, seeing how much he hates everybody."

"And vice versa, maybe he's going on somewhere else and just popped in on his way."

"I hope so, look out, he's coming over."

"Hi Tim, hi Chris, just thought I'd pop in and wish you all the best, can I get you a drink?"

"That would be great, we're both on lager". He looked at Chris's still almost full pint and flicked a quick smile at him before taking a large gulp of his own. The offer clearly hadn't been to both of them, but getting one over on the boss is always a good feeling. Lagrange turned towards the bar and took out his wallet. The brief, stilted and awkward conversation that followed seemed to last an age, the smallest of small talk; weather, traffic, what was coming in at Potters in the next few weeks. Bev and Deb made a timely return to rescue them just at the point Chris thought he was going to have to abandon Tim on the pretext of going to the toilet. Leaving Lagrange to talk to the people on the other side of him they made their escape.

"No man left behind", Bev intoned in a gruff impression of a combat soldier. They laughed and moved in on a recently abandoned table, setting down their drinks and claiming an orphan chair from a neighbouring table.

We must look like the most improbable group of friends anywhere Chris thought to himself, but friends they undoubtedly were. Stirred by Tim's offer of help he wondered why he had not asked more of them when he had needed it most, but he knew the answer before he had even asked himself – it was because he hadn't needed to. Over the last two months they had always been there with him, in the background, checking in, being nearby and watching and listening for him. They had been ready for when he couldn't manage alone, but had given him the time and space to do what he had to do. Giving him his privacy, and the time he needed had been the most generous thing they could do.

He looked over at Bev, again deep in baby related conversation, he wondered what was on her mind right now. Maybe it was his turn to step up and be a friend. He decided he would make time tomorrow to ask what was up, if it was any of his business, and offer what help he could, because that was what friends were for after all.

Scanning the busy room he saw Kiera, her full make up, sequinned top and tight skirt showed she had made the effort to dress for the occasion. Next to her, slumped in his chair and looking at his phone, was the lad from the pub – the boy racer who collected her from work most days. His jeans, Nike t-shirt and baseball cap showed he had made no such effort. The petulant, bored look on his face plainly showed what he thought of being dragged along to Tim's leaving do.

For a brief moment Chris felt a pang of sympathy for Kiera, but only the briefest moment; he was still not that far along the road of forgiveness or forgetting. He looked back towards Lagrange just in time to see him instructing the barman to turn the music off. It stopped abruptly, mid-song, leaving a void filled by too-loud conversations trailing off and people looking around to see what had happened.

Lagrange tapped the edge of his glass with a pen and cleared his throat in an exaggerated and overdramatic fashion to draw attention to himself then stood on a chair that he had procured from somewhere and raised an arm in the air to ensure that people were looking in the right direction.

"Oh my God, he's going to make a fucking speech." Chris muttered to himself under his breath. Evidently, he did not do this as quietly as he thought, Bev, Tim and Deb looked over at him smirking, sniggering and rolling their eyes.

The room quietened as the remaining conversations ground to a halt, everyone now looking towards Lagrange expectantly. He cleared his throat again, less extravagantly this time, and started to speak;

"Ladies and gentlemen, colleagues, co-workers,"

Chris did not think anyone present considered Lagrange to be either a colleague or a co-worker.

"it's great to see you all here this evening, and it's lovely to be here and to have a chance to say goodbye and good luck to Tim, who has given so many years of hard work to the company."

All eyes now turned towards Tim, who looked surprised, awkward and embarrassed. He took a swig from his pint and acknowledged the onlooking faces of the assembled group by raising his free hand briefly to shoulder height.

"I know he's going to be missed by all of us, it certainly won't be the same in the yard without him and his expertise and experience keeping everything running smoothly."

'As if Lagrange would have any idea what Tim actually did in the yard – idiot,' thought Chris.

"I'm sure you would all like to join me in raising a glass to him and wishing him the best of luck."

Glasses were duly raised and calls of 'good luck' and 'to Tim' rippled around the room.

"I would like to present you with this as a token of GardenCo's appreciation for your hard work and effort."

Lagrange stepped down from his chair and produced an envelope from his jacket pocket that he walked over and handed to Tim amidst a smattering of applause.

Chris guessed it would be GardenCo vouchers, the same as they gave Jill when she left, bloody cheapskates.

Now one of the yard team who had been organising a collection for Tim stepped forward with an armful of ornately wrapped offerings that had been hastily produced from somewhere.

"These are from all of us Tim, good luck, we'll miss you."

To enthusiastic response she handed him the wine bottle shaped bag, a small box and envelope and passed a bunch of flowers to Deb who had moved up beside Tim. She nudged him and nodded her head.

"Thanks. I'm not much of a one for making speeches, so I won't. But thanks for coming, it's been good working with you all."

The claps and cheers that sounded at the end of Tim's brief speech should have signalled an end to the formalities, but it seemed that Lagrange had not finished yet, he climbed back onto his chair and waited for the clapping to stop with his arm raised in the air once more. The noise subsided and he was, once more, the centre of attention.

"I know we'll all be sad to see Tim leave, I don't want to hijack his leaving do…"

'You just have, you idiot,' Chris thought crossly.

"…but I just wanted to take the opportunity while we're all together to give you some more news. I'm sorry to have to tell you all that I will be leaving in six weeks to take over as manager of a different GardenCo centre."

There was a momentary silence, followed by a slightly hesitant round of applause that quickly petered out.

"I can't tell you yet who my replacement will be, but I'm sure you'll make them as welcome as you made me."

'I'm pretty sure we can do better than that,' Chris was pleasantly surprised nonetheless.

He raised his glass and took a drink, this was mirrored by the room.

"Ok, well don't stay up too late, see you all tomorrow morning."

Groans now as he stepped down off his chair once more and nodded to the barman to turn the music back on. A general hubbub of surprised conversation restarted as everyone took in this new and unexpected piece of news.

Chris watched Lagrange as he stood awkwardly by the bar for a moment, waiting to see if people would rush forward to shake his hand, wish him good luck, tell him how much he'd be missed. One or two souls did, but you wouldn't call it a rush. He finished his drink, put the empty glass on the bar and picked out a route to the door.

Chris felt a pang of guilt, maybe he should have gone over and wished him well. But he didn't, and he didn't want to be a hypocrite any more than the other occupants of the room. He leaned back into his chair, his previous good feeling now diminished. He let the new information sink in, glad that he would no longer have to work under someone he had so little respect for. But who would be replacing Lagrange? Surely it couldn't be worse – could it?

The room became noisier again, the music restarted and people mixed in fluctuating groups, browsing the now diminished buffet table, hoovering up the remaining sausage rolls and ham sandwiches and ferrying pints of beer and glasses of wine around the busy room. The laughter, noise and music surrounded Chris and swallowed him up, overwhelming him. He felt an urge to get out, leaving his drink he slalomed to the door and emerged in the quiet street.

The streetlights were now on, their lamps surrounded by a wispy corona of mist. The neighbouring shops were shuttered up for the night and the pavement showed the stains and detritus from the day, waiting for the early morning cleaning crew to come along and revive them while everybody else slept.

A small group of smokers gathered by the light of the pub window next to a bucket of butt filled sand, talking in hushed tones as their plumes of smoke twisted their way through the yellow light as they disappeared into the darkness. The noise from inside had followed Chris out, but now it was muted and distant. A faraway sound of a car driving too fast and an echoing shout as someone called out to a friend.

To his left were Kiera and her boyfriend, she had her back to Chris blocking his view of the boyfriend. Although he could not see him clearly, he could tell from the tone of his voice and the way he was gesticulating that he was impatient, maybe even angry. The words were inaudible and lost, the meaning was not.

Chris leaned back against the doorpost, breathing in the night air, distant and dislocated from what was happening around him. He didn't know what he was doing here, he only came because he didn't want to disappoint Tim, now he'd shown his face surely he could go home, have a cup of tea, listen to some decent music, write his neglected blog; probably about how much he hated parties.

Baby talk had been an immersive experience for Bev. Deb's excitement was palpable, along with the just below the surface nerves. This was familiar territory for Bev, although not recent. Her memories from two decades ago were still fresh, some things stay with you for a lifetime, waiting for the right trigger to emerge and set them free again. Deb soaked up Bev's description of childbirth and motherhood, eager to gain as much knowledge as she could about the world she was about to enter. Bev judiciously glossed over some of the less glamorous moments, Deb didn't really need to know about them right now, she focussed instead on the moments of magic and joy that she had ahead of her.

Tim came back to the table, having been released (or escaped) from the group of people he had been standing with. Bev looked around to see Chris on his way to the door.

"I'm just going to catch up with Chris, see you in a bit."

Deb and Tim were busy debating whether Tim had had enough to drink yet, they acknowledged her as she followed Chris to the door. Leaving the pub for a quieter, cooler world she saw Kiera and her boyfriend walking off, she was following two steps behind him. The smokers by the window glanced up briefly and then went back to their conversations. Bev was pretty sure that at least two of them had only been inside the pub to collect dinks. Chris was standing by the door, lost in his own reverie he hadn't noticed Bev yet.

"Penny for them?"

"Eh?"

"Penny for your thoughts."

"Huh, they're not worth that much. Sorry, I was in a little world of my own there."

"You okay?"

"Yeah, good news about Lagrange eh? I won't miss him."

"I'm with you on that, who do you think they'll get to replace him?"

"Don't know, can't be worse though, can it?"

"Probably not. Do you want another drink?"

"No, I'm thinking of calling it a night. I'm done."

"Lightweight."

"I know, one drink and I'm anybody's…"

"…two and you're everybody's."

They both laugh at this familiar shared joke.

"Do you want to share a cab back?"

"You don't have to leave."

"No, but I'm knackered. I've not been sleeping well."

Bev had spent most of her time when she wasn't distracted worrying about Dave, where he was, what was going to happen.

Polly had stayed at home and between them they had called everybody and anybody that they could think of that might know his whereabouts, to no avail. They had talked until late in the night about what else they could do, but had got no further forward.

"You look tired, is everything okay? Is there anything I can do?"

"Thanks Chris, I don't think so. Dave's gone and I don't know where he is."

"Why? What happened?"

"We had a row, it was silly really, I just want to know he's okay is all."

"Oh Bev, you should have said something, or taken some time off."

"I'd have just been sat around waiting, it's best to keep busy sometimes."

"I know what you mean, but if there's anything I can do just ask."

"I will, thanks."

"Come on, we'll go and say goodbye to Tim and I'll call a cab."

*

Chris levered himself out of the cab.

"Do you want to come in for a coffee?"

"No thanks, I need to try and get some sleep."

"Fair enough, see you tomorrow."

She watched him limp and shuffle up to his door where he waved over his shoulder as he fitted the key in the lock and the cab moved on to complete its journey.

Tim had been predictably emotional when they left, hugging them both and repeatedly thanking them for coming, for working with him, for helping him and anything else he could find to sing their praises about. While they gently tried to break away Deb passed him a glass of water, putting it in his hand.

161

"Drink this, you'll thank me tomorrow."

"It looks a bit weak."

"Just drink it funny man."

"Okay love, whatever you say."

A mock stern look from Deb, followed by another round of goodbyes and then they were in the cab which arrived moments after they stepped out of the pub.

Now, as the cab turned into her road, Bev wished she had taken up Chris on his offer of coffee. Polly had gone to her boyfriends for the night, not wanting to be alone in the house. Which, of course, meant that Bev would now be the one who was on her own. Maybe for the best, the evening had been good and she had enjoyed talking to Deb about babies and all the warm fuzzy memories, she could sit and look through the baby albums with a cup of tea without embarrassing Polly.

The cab pulled up outside the house, as Bev passed a fiver to the driver she looked towards the house and saw that Dave's car was parked behind hers on the drive.

CHAPTER 28

LATER

Poquelin was waiting in the bedroom. The lights were turned off, leaving just the glow of the computer monitor to illuminate the room. It reflected onto one half of his face and body, leaving the rest of him in darkness, blending with the shadows as he sat on the desk next to the computer.
"Take a seat."

He indicated the chair that had been pulled away from the desk and set alone in the middle of the floor. Chris walked to it, resigned, and sat down. He looked at the screen which was currently flickering with white specks on a blue background.

"Is this going to take long?"

"As long as it takes."

"I'm pretty knackered."

"Shut up and watch."

Poquelin snapped his claw-like fingers at the monitor and it flicked into life, a jerky, grainy image of a familiar corridor. The view changed as the unseen camera operator moved along the corridor and stopped outside a door that Chris had hoped he would never see again.

"That's enough now, stop it."

"It's never enough. Sit down and shut up."

Chris had started to rise, at the tone of Poquelin's voice he sat back down. On the screen the door was opening to a sterile white room containing a single bed surrounded by a chair and side table and a wall full of trollies loaded with medical equipment; tubes, gleaming stainless-steel instruments and packets of dressings waiting to be opened and used. Chris turned his head away and closed his eyes.

"Please stop."

"No."

Unable to help himself Chris continued to watch the flickering image on the screen. A nurse had entered the room and was busy checking temperatures and arranging equipment on a trolley. He watched as the inert body on the bed was rolled about, unresisting, as various cleaning, feeding and grooming procedures were administered by the disinterested nurse. All things he had seen numerous times before as he sat quietly out of the way and waited for them to leave before he moved his chair back beside the bed and talked about his day, how the garden was looking and the mundanities of life outside the hospital.

Occasionally, and less frequently as time went on, he would get a moment of recognition. Their eyes would meet or there would be the faintest flicker of a smile in response to something he had said. Once her hand had reached out and laid gently on top of his, squeezing gently. Then her eyes had closed again, if they had ever been fully open to start with, and a single jewel-like teardrop sat glistening in the corner of her eye.

"I can't do this."

"Tch!"

A loud click and the picture changed, now it was his sitting room as it had looked before he redecorated. The horses were back on the wall, the antimacassars all in place, every ornament and trinket correctly positioned. Chris saw himself, slumped on the settee with his eyes closed and a cold cup of tea at his side. On the coffee table were a selection of leaflets and booklets that the hospital staff had given him. He hadn't looked at them yet, the titles had been enough to disabuse him of the notion that he would get any pleasure or enjoyment from them;

'What to do when a loved one dies.'

'Living with Grief.'

Not that he supposed he was meant to enjoy reading them, but one thing at a time – this was not the time.

Although there was no sound with this film, he knew the moment the phone rang. The Chris on the screen blinked his eyes open and jerked upright. He watched himself move quickly across the room and hold the receiver to his ear, he moved his mouth then dropped the phone back into its holder and slumped into the armchair closest to him, just as Chris had known he would.

Back in the here and now Chris wiped away the tears that were rolling unashamedly down his face.

"Can we stop now please?"

Poquelin clicked his fingers again and grinned a sharp-toothed smile as the screen returned to its fuzzy blue default.

"Why would you make me watch that?"

"You needed to see it, you've been hiding away and pretending things didn't happen, just like you have done all your life."

"You don't know me."

"I do, better than you think. You're always running away from things, avoiding the issues."

"That's not true, I don't do that."

"You do, it's what you always do. You revel in your victimhood; you're so wrapped up in it you can't see the good things that are happening all around you. That's fine, but if you're going to be angry be properly angry – set the world on fire, burn it down to the charred and blackened lump it deserves to be."

"You don't understand, I just want to keep myself to myself, if you knew what it was like to look like this;"

He indicated his ruined face and shortened leg with a wave of his hand.

"ARE YOU FUCKING KIDDING ME?" Poquelin roared, he stood on the desk, spreading his wings to their fullest extent. Suddenly he looked enormous, Chris could see that the wings were ragged and frayed, the teeth chipped and cracked and the limbs so nobbled and bulbous that everything seemed to be fighting against itself in an effort to straighten out.

"If I knew what it was like? Look at me! LOOK! You with your limp and fading scars, you could pass as normal in poor light – I'd need a fucking full eclipse. Your friends don't even notice anymore, I'm not welcome anywhere, I'm a monster. 'If you knew what it was like…' idiot!"

Silence embraced them, then a squelching, rustling sound as Poquelin folded himself back up and sat back on the edge of the desk. Chris watched mutely, had he just been torn off a strip? By a monster? In his own house?

"It's different, you know it is. I don't revel in it, I hate it. Why would I want to look like this?"

"You do, you won't let things go – and that's alright – just own it."

"It's not true."

Chris realised how petulant he was beginning to sound; he recognised a kernel of truth in what Poquelin was saying. Since school he had kept away from other people as much as he could, in spite of this he had still found friends, like Bev and Tim. Not a lot of friends, but some people who accepted him for who and what he was. Not wanting to lose face he doubled down."

166

"People just feel sorry for me, they're sympathy friends. They want to tick the box next the other boxes for black, Jewish and gay friends. I'm everyone's pet charity."

As soon as the words left his mouth, he knew that he had gone beyond petulant, into the realms of churlish and querulous. He knew how stupid it made him sound. Clearly Poquelin knew too, he looked at Chris with an expression that would have included raised eyebrows if he had any. Chris's voice lowered, he looked at his hands which he was rubbing together as he picked at his nails.

"It's not my fault."

"Whose is it then? Your dad for leaving? Your Mum for letting you fall in the fire? The school for kicking you out? The doctors for not being able to fix you? Whose fault is it?"

"Nobody's, it's just one of those things, it just happened."

"Except it didn't, you made all your own choices, you decided to be the way you are, the person you are. Well, now it's time to choose again, are you going to carry on pushing people away, hiding, being angry?"

"People don't like me, they shun me."

"More self-pity, get over it. Look at this;"

Another click of the fingers and the computer screen reanimated, this time in full sharp colour with a steady camera.

It was his old school hall, the rows of plastic chairs full of students in polyester blazers and red and white ties with teachers policing the ends of the rows. The stage was full of the headmaster, his lackies and two tables covered with cheap plastic trophies and reams of certificates. Chris groaned out loud, it was prize day.

The camera work was very slick and professional, more than compensating for the lack of sound. It was clear what was going on from the close up of the headmaster, shaved pink chin and close-cropped hair, intoning names silently. The picture would then pan out and show the rows of clapping students and staff as someone –

167

now zoom in on them – stood up and walked to the front to collect their award – close up on their smiling but slightly embarrassed face.

Chris knew what was coming and wanted to look away, wanted to run out of the room and hide. He also knew it would do no good, that he would have to see this through or Poquelin would find a way to make him. Anger began to mix with the smorgasbord of emotions he was experiencing.

On the screen Trevor Roberts went to collect his commendation for excellent maths work. Trevor had been in the same maths group as Chris, cheerful, freckly with a wild mop of curly hair. He had earned his maths award through hard work and a natural affinity for numbers and problem solving, he was never happier than when he was presented with a question that had flummoxed the rest of the class.

After maths prodigy Trevor had shaken hands with the headteacher he turned with a beaming smile and waved to his twin sister who would be following him to the stage shortly. The same wayward curly hair, but longer, and a preference to writing rather than numbering. She would get the essay writing prize for a report she had written for the school magazine. Richly deserved in Chris's opinion, anyone who can bring a chess match to life – make it exciting even - has truly earned their prize.

Now it was the part that Chris had been dreading. Although he hadn't wanted to watch, he now couldn't tear his eyes away. As Sally Roberts left the stage the sound started abruptly, loud and echoey. The applause petered out and the headmaster consulted the piece of paper in his hand. Looking up he intoned Chris's name in his slightly nasal Welsh accent as he scanned the room to see where Chris was going to appear from.

Chris knows full well what happens next, the humiliation of having every person in the room laughing at him, laughing at the way he looked, the way he moved. The universal mockery and contempt were burned into his memory even after all these years.

As Mr Thomas finished reading his name there was a minor commotion at the front of the hall, a flurry of movement and a ripple of people turning to look and see what was going on. At the epicentre of the disturbance somebody stood up, Chris had just stood and was edging to the end of the row to come forward. He had a clear view as somebody appeared in a rubber Freddy Krueger mask that they had evidently just put on, they limped in an exaggerated fashion along the front of the hall in front of the stage. Chris paused, frozen, then when everybody's attention was focussed on what was happening at the front he continued to the end of the row, out of the door and he ran.

The camera had followed him to the door and filmed him as he lurched away from himself, away from assembly, school and ridicule. He had never returned to school after that. As he rounded the corner the camera turned back to the hall full of laughing staff and students.

Except it wasn't.

There was a deathly hush as people looked at one another unsure what to do. Mrs Douglas, the music teacher, got up and walked past the camera into the corridor in a belated attempt to find Chris. Mr Thomas had come down from the stage and gripped the upper arm of Freddy Kreuger with one hand while he roughly removed the mask with his free hand.

"My office now!"

He did not raise his voice. The low growl of his tone carried clearly and left nobody in any doubt as to the seriousness of the trouble the offender was in, Janet Cox's smirk disappeared quickly as she looked around and found that the howls of laughter she had been expecting from her hilarious prank had not materialised. The silence was now being displaced with a low murmuring, someone in the middle of the hall called out;

"Stupid cow."

There was ripple of assent, the comment went uncontested by members of staff as Janet Cox was led from the hall by one of Mr

Thomas's henchmen. Mr Thomas, red-faced, reclaimed the stage and attempted to restart the event. But now the feelgood factor had clearly gone, the special day had turned sour and he hurried through the remainder, keen to get back to his office and deal with the matter at hand. The sound faded out, leaving the prizegiving playing out silently on the screen.

"They didn't laugh."

"Of course they didn't, who would laugh at a thing like that?"

"I thought they all did."

"You'd have known if you ever went back."

"How could I have gone back after that?"

"People wanted to see you; check you were okay. They were upset too."

"They weren't as upset as me."

"You'd be surprised, the Roberts twins both cried when they got home. You would've known if you'd ever read any of the letters or cards people sent you."

He hadn't, of course. His mum had passed them to him but they had all been posted straight into the bin unopened.

"She got expelled."

"Good."

"Her friends all started to ditch her after that."

"Good."

A heavy silence hung in the air as all this new information was absorbed. Or was it new? Chris thought he had suspected or known these things all along. Whatever, it was history now.

"I'm going to bed."

"Go on then, busy day tomorrow."

This acquiescence from Poquelin was new, Chris didn't question it, he took off his shoes, socks and jeans and buried himself in the bed while the little monster sat quietly and watched. As Chris settled there was a soft click and the room was left in darkness.

CHAPTER 29

LATER THAN THAT

The doorbell was ringing repeatedly, sending its sharp message around the house and into Chris's room. He looked at his clock, 6.25, why the fuck would anyone be ringing the doorbell at 6.25? Whoever it was clearly wasn't taking no for an answer, the bell rang again. Chris pulled his dressing gown from the back of the door and wrapped it around himself as he made his way to the door, which had just summoned him again.

"I'm coming."

Bev stood on the doorstep, red-eyed and looking anxious;

"I'm sorry, I'm really sorry to wake you up so early."

"What's up? No, sorry, come in. Put the kettle on, I'll be right back, I'm bursting. You know where everything is right?"

"I'm so sorry, I didn't know where else to go."

"It's fine, just give me a minute."

Bev came in as Chris hurried up the stairs. She went straight to the kitchen, as instructed, put the kettle on and got out some mugs. Over the sound of the boiling water she heard the toilet flush and some bumping and banging from upstairs. Moments later Chris reappeared in a pair of hastily located joggers and a sweatshirt.

"Tea or coffee?"

"Eh? Oh, tea please. What on earth is up Bev? Are you okay?"

Bev heard the concern in his voice and was embarrassed at having woken him up so early, but she wasn't ready to share just yet. She kept to the subject in hand;

"Tea, sure. I'm having coffee – I need it. Where's the sugar?"

Chris reached it out of the cupboard and placed it on the counter along with the other drink making materials.

"Has something happened?"

"No. Well, yes but I need a moment, is that okay?"

"No problem, do you want some breakfast? I've got some eggs and bacon."

"I don't want to put you out."

"I'm going to make some for myself."

"Okay, yes please. I didn't think I was hungry, but actually now you've offered I'm ravenous."

"Excellent, me too. I didn't really have much of a go at the buffet last night."

"Me neither, can I help?"

"No, it's all in hand."

Chris had already reached out the ancient, blackened, cast-iron frying pan, a 'family heirloom' they had used to joke. He put it on the hob and soon bacon and eggs were sizzling in the hot fat. Some doorstep slices of bread, plates and cutlery completed the preparations as Bev sipped her sweet black coffee and watched Chris gently lift the eggs onto the plates and put them on the table along with some butter and ketchup. He had respectfully not asked any more about why she was there, and although she knew she would have to tell him soon she was glad of the moment of normality to collect her thoughts. She knew she had made the right choice coming here, although she felt bad for turning up and dragging him out of bed at this ungodly hour.

In truth, she only half knew herself why she had come to see Chris. She could have gone and sat in the park, or found an early opening café or MacDonalds. But she had wanted some privacy, a place away from the world. Chris had always been patient and kind to her in the past, and even though it felt like she was taking advantage of him he had not let her down. He fished the toast out from under the grill and they ate, appetites fuelled by the distinctive smells of a fried breakfast. She tried to think of a time that Dave had ever made breakfast for her, but drew a blank, she started to cry.

"Sorry."

"Nothing to be sorry for." He passed a piece of kitchen roll to fulfil the function of a tissue. "Eat up, while it's still hot, nothing worse than congealed eggs."

There are worse things though Bev thought, way worse. Nevertheless, she dried her eyes and started eating She quickly found her appetite was indeed there, with a vengeance. Before long they were facing each other with fresh tea and coffee in front of them and the plates, smeared with yellow and red streaks, on the counter waiting to be washed.

"Dave's left me."

"He called back then?"

"No, he was there when I got back, packing. He thought I wouldn't be back until later."

"Did he say why? Or is that none of my business?"

"No, I owe you an explanation. He didn't want to talk, but I insisted we did. We talked all night – then I came here because I couldn't bear to be in the house while he collected the rest of his stuff and I couldn't think where else to go. I'm so sorry."

"Stop apologising, I told you, it's okay."

"I know, but I feel bad. You were asleep, and none of this is your problem."

"Well, I had to get up anyway, someone was…."

"Ringing the doorbell." Bev finished for him.

They both managed a smile at this old, but not yet retired, joke.

"He's moving in with a man he plays golf with."

"What? Flatmates, bachelor pad type of thing?"

He knew it was precisely not 'that type of thing' the moment the words left his mouth, Bev's face crumpled again. She felt the tears welling up and reached for another piece of kitchen roll which Chris had conveniently left on the table.

"All those years, and I never knew, I feel so stupid. I feel like it's all my fault, it's humiliating, what will everyone think?"

"They'll think Dave's a dick for not saying something before."

"He said he's always felt like this, he only went along with what was expected of him, by family, friends. He thought he would start to feel different, but then he met Derek at the club and realised he didn't, and never had." Oh my God, I really am a golf widow now aren't I?"

"I guess so." They both managed a half smile. "Didn't you have any idea?"

"He'd never been that interested in me, I just thought it was me, that maybe if I tried a bit harder."

"I'm sorry Bev, this must be awful for you. Does Polly know yet?"

"No, I'll tell her later, Dave won't, says it would be too hard. Like it's going to be easy for me."

"She'll understand, kids today are more open than we were. It'll still be a shock though I guess."

"I'll tell her as gently as I can, but it would be better if it came from Dave. He's such a bloody coward. God, I'm so tired I can hardly think, do you suppose he's finished packing up yet?"

"Go and have a lie down here, there's a spare bed made up. I'll tell them at work that you're not coming in, I'm sure Kiera can cover it she's got the hang of things now."

"I couldn't, I've already imposed too much. I'm so sorry Chris, dumping all this on you."

"Don't be. Go and get some sleep, you'll feel better for it."

"Maybe just for a little bit, are you sure you don't mind?"

"I wouldn't have offered if I did. Go on, I'll tidy up here and go to work, it's nearly time to get moving anyway. I'll square things up with Lagrange."

"Thank you, thank you so much."

Bev didn't think she would be able to sleep with so much to occupy her thoughts. She slipped off her shoes, lay down and fell into a deep sleep.

Chris washed up and then went upstairs to get dressed properly. He looked in on Bev, fast asleep. He thought he had never felt so out of depth in a conversation in his life, he had no idea what he should have said, or if what he had said had been wrong or right. He left a note on the bedside table and gently covered Bev with a blanket.

*

The unfamiliar bed and strangeness of the room confused Bev momentarily, it took a few seconds for her to get her bearings. Once she did everything came rushing back, squeezing into every corner of her waking consciousness as she tried to decide what she needed to do and what order to do it in. She sat on the edge of the bed and read the note that she found on the bedside table;

Bev,

I hope some sleep has helped a bit, please make yourself at

home and stay as long as you need to. It's fine if you want to

meet Polly here, there is plenty of milk. Biscuits are in the tin.

Speak later

Chris.

She folded the note, then folded the blanket and went to the bathroom. Examining her reflection in the mirror over the sink she saw all her years in the bags under her eyes, the smudged traces of last night, make-up smeared, hair shot with traces of grey and sticking out at a range of impossible angles. She straightened herself as best she could with the materials available then went back onto the landing. She looked into Chris's room through the open door.

Two yellow eyes looked back at her.

Bev stepped back with a start, then looked again. The bedside light had been left on, a weird reflection of this had cast two pinpricks of light onto the computer monitor, bright but not yellow and definitely not eyes. Still, a shiver ran down her spine and she hastily went downstairs and made coffee, the bitter taste and strong smell started to revive her from her disorientation and she started to get her thoughts in order. She knew what she had to do first, she called Polly and left a message for her to meet her at home as soon as she could.

There was nothing obviously missing when she walked through the front door, no glaring voids or empty spaces, but still the house felt emptier than it had before. It was only when she looked into the office that the changes started appearing; there were some gaps on the bookshelf and the broken drawer was empty. She was glad she had kept a hold of the notebook with all the passwords, who knew when she might need them again? There was a post-it note on the computer screen with a forwarding address for Dave, she didn't even bother to look where it was. Upstairs the bathroom shelf had been stripped of shaving accoutrements and the wardrobe was left open with a large space where he had taken some of his essential clothes. His bedside table was cleared of everything, leaving only dust and a faint coffee ring.

'He could have bloody wiped it down.'

Downstairs the sound of a key in the lock carried upstairs. Bev hurried down to meet Polly as she let herself in, coming face to face with her at the bottom of the stairs. She took one look at Polly, standing with her blue backpack in one hand and her coat in the other, and burst into tears.

"Mum, what's up? You look awful, what's happened? I got here as quick as I could."

"Do I look that bad?"

"You don't look great."

"It was a long night."

Where's Dad, is he okay?"

"He's fine. Come in, put your stuff down and I'll get the kettle on, I've only just got in myself. I'll tell you everything once we've got that sorted."

Before long Bev sat at the table, across from Polly, mugs in hand, in an echo of the earlier conversation with Chris. This time the explanation, having been practised and mulled over, was more succinct. Polly listened without interrupting, although the expression on her face told Bev all she needed to know – it would be some time before Polly and Dave had any cosy father daughter time again.

She finished by telling Polly how she had gone to Chris's while Dave finished packing, Polly abandoned her tea and came round the table to hug Bev. The physical contact was enough to set Bev off crying again, which in turn released the floodgates for Polly. Eventually they regained enough composure for Polly to ask;

"What are we going to do now?"

"What do you mean?" Bev had not thought much beyond the here and now.

"I mean the house, can we still live here?"

"I don't know, I mean it's in his name but I don't think he can kick us out – can he?"

"I don't know."

"I guess I need to find a solicitor."

"Never mind that for now, I've got a better idea."

Polly outlined her plan. Bev looked shocked.

"We can't do that."

"We can, and we will."

The bonfire was flickering orange and red in the afternoon sun, smoke drifting up in swirling dark plumes into the watery blue afternoon sky. Bev still felt there had been an element of petty spitefulness in the ransacking of the house for Dave's uncollected belongings, but had to admit it felt good, both symbolic and cathartic. It was clearly both for Polly too, who was poking the fire with the melted rubber handle of a putter. For the first time in days she felt something other than sadness and fear, it was a creeping sense of newly acquired freedom.

"Shall we get something to eat?" she hadn't had anything since the morning fry up and her stomach was starting to complain loudly.

"Good idea, you put something on while I go to the shop and get a bottle of wine or two."

"Anything you fancy?"

"Something with chips."

They both smiled at this, 'good' thought Bev as she rummaged in the freezer.

*

It was a long day at work. Lagrange left him alone and Kiera was efficient and organised. Chris had plenty to get on with, which kept him occupied, in spite of this he couldn't stop his thoughts from wandering to Bev after their early breakfast. He hoped she had found Polly and that they were not too upset, though God knows, they should be. He tried to imagine what an awful shock it must have been, Bev really didn't deserve that. He wanted to ring and check she was okay, but didn't want to intrude at a difficult time.

Eventually the day wound down and Chris was in his car listening to the Meteors thrash through a selection of rockabilly classics. He considered driving past Bev's, but again decided that now might not be the best time. She probably had a lot to deal with, the last thing they would need would be him bothering them right now.

*

Bev and Polly had eaten, chips – as requested, and some burgers. They had opened a bottle of wine which Polly was working her way through, Bev was nursing one small glass'

"I'm too tired to drink really, it'll just knock me straight out."

They looked at Polly's open laptop while they decided what they needed Google to tell them, dozens of questions swirled in Bev's mind, questions she had never needed to know the answer to before. Bev wanted to make sense of what might happen next.

'How do I get a divorce?'

'What happens to the house?'

'Will I have enough money?'

'What happens if he wants to come back?'

'Should I change the locks?'

And so on and so on.

Together they trawled, scrolled, read and bookmarked away on the laptop. Bev was reassured to find that she wouldn't be left destitute, would have no trouble getting a divorce, and if Dave cooperated everything could be sorted fairly quickly and she could move on. If he did not, according to one forum, she was entitled to remove his testicles. Bev and Molly were pretty sure this had no basis in law, but still giggled at some of the comments and suggestions from scorned and abandoned women. Bev was glad the hurt she was feeling was a shared hurt with many other women who were victims of circumstance.

Further research, using the book of secret codes and passwords, gave more good news. Years of frugality, scrimping and saving, making do and doing without meant the mortgage was nearly paid up. There was money put aside in separate savings accounts that she had not known about, but that their research had shown them she was entitled to a share of. They found the number of a local solicitor and Bev promised Polly that she would call first thing tomorrow morning.

*

Tea was a cursory affair, comprising mostly of 'things' from the freezer. Chris turned the music up loud, letting Carter USM wash through the house as he moved restlessly from room to room, looking for something to do. Bev had left a note on the kitchen table;

Thanks Chris,

Sorry I put all that on you, and so early in the morning.

I will make it up to you some time.

I'll call later

Bev x

He wished she would, just so he could know she was okay and that Polly was looking after her. He still resisted the urge to call first, not knowing if this was the right thing to do, but sticking with his instinct that it was.

He singly failed to find anything meaningful to occupy himself. At one point he sat at his computer, idly flicking through comments on his blog but having no inclination to respond to any of the vitriol or add any new thoughts to his output. The music finished downstairs, sending silence through the rooms and he found himself idly thinking the unthinkable and wishing Poquelin would appear, at least then there would be something to do, someone to talk to. He locked the screen and went back to his tour of the house in search of entertainment.

He flicked through TV channels, but nothing fitted his mood, he wasn't even sure what would at this point. He browsed through the collection of jigsaws in the under stairs cupboard, now he looked at them he wasn't quite sure why they hadn't gone to the charity shop with the rest of the unwanted things. Next time, this weekend he would have a second, more ruthless clear out and get rid of some more clutter. Not today though.

He looked at the faded spines of the photo albums, neatly arranged in chronological order on the bookshelf. He was tempted to start flicking through, taking a trip down memory lane. Not that it would be much of a trip, for a start there where very few photos of his younger, deformed self. Fair enough, who would want a picture of that when you had to look at it every day? He knew there were pictures trapped in there that he would want to see, but not now, not so soon after the funeral.

He picked up a long out of print copy of Chandler Brossard's 'The Bold Saboteurs' from further along the shelf. Worn and faded from being read and re-read so many times, reading about George's struggles and confusion had resonated with him on some level and he kept revisiting the book at intervals to remind himself how he had felt, and wallow in some self-pity and righteous indignation.

Definitely not a book for today though, he put it back and ran his fingers along the spines of the other books hoping something would call out to him or inspire him. It was definitely not a reading evening. With a sigh he succumbed to the inevitable, he picked up his jacket and keys, checked he had his wallet and phone and left the house.

Roger greeted him as he approached the bar, he had already started pouring the drink when he saw Chris come through the door.

"Evening Chris, how's things?"

"Yeah, all good, and you?"

"You know, busy."

He looked around the room at the occupied tables near the back of the pub. The usual selection of youngsters in trainers and caps that had been there on previous visits. Amongst them was Kiera, sitting looking fed-up while her boyfriend was busy multi-tasking, simultaneously texting, talking to the man on his right and paying no attention whatsoever to Kiera.

Chris sat away from them and sipped at his pint, one gulp at a time, quietly lost in his own thoughts and checking his phone occasionally. Nobody paid him any attention, but by degrees he started to notice what was going on in his line of sight. People would come into the pub, stop at the bar to buy a drink and head straight for the tables at the back. Some people just headed directly to the back tables, bypassing Roger altogether. Most did not stay longer than it took to finish their drink or make a quick visit to the toilets before leaving. There was nothing discrete about the handing over of money or the passing of packets under the table and Kiera's boyfriend seemed to be very much the centre of attention.

He decided one drink would be enough, that he would go home and do one of the things that had seemed so unappealing an hour ago. He drained his glass and took it to the bar.

"What's going on with that lot?" He nodded to the tables.

"Don't worry, it's being dealt with," Roger made a face that somehow conveyed that he was being deliberately cryptic and oblique, "it'll all be back to normal soon, can't say any more than that right now."

"Fair enough, see you somewhere, have a good night."

"Yeah, you too Chris, look after yourself."

He took himself out of the pub just as a group of smokers shoved past him on their way back inside. The noise from inside drifted through the open door, then became muffled as the door swung shut. He looked to his right and saw, in a replication of the previous evening, Kiera and her boyfriend arguing. The feeling of déjà vu was short lived, as Chris watched the boyfriend swung his hand at Kiera's head, the sound of the impact carried to Chris, along with Kiera's yelp of pain and the wordless shouting of her boyfriend, Chris was unable to make out anything with clarity, apart from the expletives – there were plenty of them.

Kiera fell to the floor and was shrinking back as he stood over her with his fists clenched. Chris knew he had to do something, calling the police would take too long, and running back into the Crown for help would eat up precious seconds. He walked briskly towards them, calling as he approached.

"Hi Kiera, are you okay there?"

The boyfriend looked at him and pointed back towards the pub.

"You - fuck off and mind your own business."

The violence implicit in the instruction made Chris's stomach lurch, he wondered if he had chosen the right option. He suddenly found that he badly needed to pee, his head kept shouting 'do it, run, get out of here.' He wasn't a fighter and there was nobody else to help, no back up. He looked down at Kiera, the side of her face was already swelling up, a trickle of blood came from her left nostril and curved around the side of her mouth. Her eyes looked back at him with a mixture of fear and pleading gratitude. He ignored his blurring vision and the rapid beating of his heart and carried on towards them.

"I told you to fuck off crip."

"I'm just checking Kiera's okay, I work with her you know?"

"Of course I fucking know who you are, take your ugly spastic face away from here."

By now Chris had reached them, he offered his hand to Kiera, clenching his neck muscles as he expected a blow to land on him at any moment. It never came, Kiera took his hand and he helped her unsteadily to her feet where she held his hand in her own small, warm fingers as she looked warily at her boyfriend. He stepped back and pointed at her;

"I'm going to get my stuff, you fucking stay here. And you," he pushed his hand into Chris's chest, forcing him to take a step backwards, "you better fuck off now, like I told you to."

He feinted a blow towards Chris's head, making him duck and take another step back, then turned and walked towards the pub. As he went he shouted back over his shoulder;

"Stay right where you are Kiera, I fucking mean it."

He went inside and Kiera turned her scared eyes towards Chris;

"Thanks, but you'd better go though, he's really mad."

"So I noticed, are you okay?"

"I'm fine."

A sudden flood of tears that ran into the smudged blood on her upper lip gave away the lie.

"What can I do? I'm scared, he's never been like this before."

At this moment fate intervened and took control of the next decision. A mini cab turned into the road, heading towards them, Chris stepped out in front of it and forced it to a halt. The driver slid down the window;

"You need to book mate, I can't take fares unless they come from control."

"I know, but it's an emergency, she's hurt look. Can you get her home?"

"I'm not supposed to."

The driver was wavering, he looked at Kiera standing anxiously beside Chris and looking nervously back towards the pub, her eye was now visibly bruised and swollen and she was still crying.

"Have you called the police?"

185

"Not yet, she's going to do it when she gets home and safe. Right now she needs to be gone from here."

"Well…"

Chris took out his wallet and made to open it.

"No, alright mate, I see what's happened, jump in love and I'll get you back home."

Chris opened the door and Kiera climbed in.

"Are you coming too?"

"No, I only live round the corner. Go on, go home and get something cold on that. And call the police to report it."

He closed the door as Kiera was thanking him and the cab started to move towards the pub. Chris turned to go towards home, but before he had taken a single step a loud shout came from behind him. He turned back to see the boyfriend outside the door watching Kiera drive by in the cab, he ran into the road behind it, shouting, but it was too late. He turned abruptly round to face in Chris's direction and shouted,

"I'm going to fucking kill you, you spastic bastard."

As he spoke he started to run in Chris's direction.

Even though he knew it would be hopeless to even try, his built up shoe and awkward gait did not lend themselves to speed, Chris began to run. He was not designed for running, and the footsteps behind him seemed to be getting closer at an alarmingly rapid rate. His heart beat faster in his panic and exertion, but it had little effect. He tried to speed up, thinking that if he could just make it to the corner he would somehow be safer. There was no logic or reasoning to this, just the blind hope, born from panic, that he could get out of this somehow. He felt like he was literally running for his life, running and fighting were not his forte, which only left one option, which was to recieve a beating.

His own breath roared and rattled in his ears as he felt himself running out of steam, inevitably slowing down, hearing the shouts and footsteps behind him as they rapidly bore down on him. He knew he had made a choice which had set this course of events in motion, and wouldn't have done it differently, but now he supposed he had to see this through to the bitter inevitable conclusion.

Once again, fate had different plans, not better, just different. As he twisted to look over his shoulder at his attacker his traitor leg gave way, sending him sprawling to the ground. He reached out his hand to break his fall and felt a sickening crunch as the impact of the pavement sent a jolt up through his wrist, elbow and arm and into his shoulder, ending there with a cracking noise. His momentum carried him forward, rolling over the collar bone that he already knew was broken, making him scream with pain.

He had not even come to a halt before he felt the weight of a foot in the small of his back, this was it, now he was going to get his promised beating - as well as falling over his own feet and damaging himself, there was nothing he could do about it. Except the second kick didn't come, it took Chris a moment to realise that he had not been kicked, in fact Kiera's boyfriend had tripped over his prone body. Chris knew this because he saw him fly forward over him, flailing wildly but unable to stop himself lunging headfirst into a lamppost. His head hit with a dull thud and his inert body fell to the ground just beyond where Chris lay. He closed his eyes and wondered what came next, the boyfriend's mates out to exact revenge he guessed. He knew this might be his only chance to get away; he gritted his teeth and braced himself for the pain of getting up from the floor and trying to get his mangled body safely home.

Then there was noise and commotion, tyres on tarmac, engines revving, car doors being swung open. Chris opened his eyes to a discotheque of blue flashing lights, a policeman stood over Kiera's boyfriend talking into his radio and beckoning a colleague over as knelt to check that he was alive. He felt a hand gently place itself on his back and turned his head to see a female police officer kneeling next to him.

"It's okay, stay still there's an ambulance on the way."

He was reassured to know that he was not going to get the pummelling that he had expected, but now another thought entered his head.

"I didn't do anything to him, he was trying to get me."

"We know, we've been watching. Now just stay still and try not to move too much, it looks like you've hurt your shoulder."

"Who's been watching? I didn't see anybody."

"You weren't supposed to, and it was the pub we were watching, not you, you just happened along at the wrong time. Or maybe it was the right time by the looks of things."

The road was awash with police cars and vans, turning his head he saw they were centred on the pub where officers in stab vests and helmets were escorting people out and into the waiting vans. The car closest to him was parked diagonally across the end of the road just ahead of him, he had so nearly made the corner. Another officer in hi viz was waving drivers past to find a different route to their destinations. Kiera's boyfriend was now groggily trying to get up, blood streamed down one side of his face as the officer tried to wrap a rough bandage around the wound and persuade him to stay on the ground. When he struggled to his feet he was asked again, less politely this time, to stay on the ground. His reluctance to follow this advice and try to get up, led to the officer signalling his watching colleague. He stepped over and together they helped him back into a sitting position while simultaneously putting on a pair of handcuffs in one quick, practised movement.

Chris lay back down and let the pain wash over him now the fear-fuelled adrenalin was starting to subside. He couldn't tell if it was seconds or minutes before another voice spoke to him, his angry shoulder and the small of his back sang about the bruises they were going to show the world tomorrow as a paramedic gently prodded and poked him. Eventually she was convinced that it was safe to move him and he was lifted gently onto a stretcher. It hurt, no way around it, every bit of him protested at every slight jiggle and bump, he would rather just stay still right where he was. Once he was resting on a padded surface with a pillow under has head and a blanket draped across him he admitted to himself that it had been worth it – probably.

He was just about to be wheeled into the back of the waiting ambulance when Roger's familiar face appeared above him, his beard creating a peculiar upside-down-head illusion from where Chris was lying.

"Oh my God mate, are you okay? I mean obviously you're not or you wouldn't be on a stretcher, but are you going to be okay?"

"I've had worse."

"I bet you have mate, I bet you have. Seriously, sorry you got mixed up in all of this crap, I couldn't say anything earlier but they've been watching the place for days. I'm not having that sort of shit going on in my pub."

"It's my own fault, I could've just walked away, I'd be home in bed by now."

"No, you did good, that toerag came back in bragging about what he'd done and what he was going to do. Looks like you sorted him out though."

"Yeah, something like that."

"Okay, we need to get going now, you need some x-rays and a bit of TLC," the paramedic gently interjected.

"You're not paying for any more drinks here," Roger informed him.

"Good, I'll be back tomorrow then."

"Hah, very funny. Look after yourself, goodnight and get well soon."

Chris let out a sigh of relief as the ambulance door closed at last, knowing that some respite from the pain would now be on its way. The Sex Pistols abruptly intruded on the peace of the cabin, Chris clumsily fished his phone from his pocket. The screen was cracked but not too badly for him to accept the incoming call from Bev.

"Hi, sorry I'm a bit busy right now, can I call you back?"

"No problem, I meant to call earlier but it went right out of my head, sorry."

"Not a problem, I'm just kind of, well...busy."

"Are you okay?"

The paramedic swiped the phone from Chris's hand and spoke into it.

"I'm sorry to butt in, we're in an ambulance so my patient isn't really supposed to be using his phone right now," she gently admonished.

"I shouldn't?"

"There are signs."

There were indeed signs now Chris looked, he apologised. The paramedic handed the phone back to him.

"Be quick," she smiled.

"Oh my God, what's happened? Are you okay?"

"I'll explain later, it's kind of a long story. I'll call you tomorrow."

"Where are you going to City?"

"There's no need....

But the phone had already gone blank. He slid it back into his pocket, laid back and closed his eyes.

CHAPTER 30

MODERN MEDICINE

From his recumbent position the world passed by at an unfamiliar and disorientating angle. In less pain now, but slightly woozy from the gas and air he had been given in the back of the ambulance; he watched signs, lights and people's chins passing by. He was familiar with the hospital, knew it far better than he had ever wanted to after too many visits. A familiar sign rolled past him directing people to the chapel.

He hurried past the sign breathless and in a panic. He had abandoned the car in the first free parking bay he had come to, he had not stopped to get a ticket and was not even certain that he had locked it. No time to go back and check now. He passed the ward names and departmental labels on a route so familiar that he didn't need to look at them to know where he was or where he was going.

Improbably young doctors with their stethoscopes worn like badges of honour, nurses in a rainbow of different coloured uniforms and scrubs designating their place, purpose and status, and patients and their families shuffled, rolled and walked down the corridor.

He kept up his pace, navigating his way around them like a human slalom course. Nobody took any notice of him; one more person having a bad day in a building full of people having bad days was hardly remarkable. The tortuously long route to his destination seemed to keep extending like a corridor in a bad dream. Finally, he arrived and turned off the corridor into the ward.

There was nobody at the nurses' station, he didn't need them anyway, he knew where to go. He opened the door and stood looking into the room, as if staring enough would change what he was seeing. The bed was empty. Not just empty, but stripped bare. Two orderlies were wiping surfaces and cleaning everything in sight. On the side was a pile of neatly folded, white, crisp bed linen. On the floor a pile of crumpled linen in bags waiting to be tied up and taken away. One of the orderlies glanced up and smiled before going back to her cleaning. He continued to stand in the doorway, not knowing what to say or what to do next. Still slightly panting and looking around as if by some extraordinary chain of events he had ended up in the wrong place.

The sharp smell of disinfectant, the sort you only get in hospitals, the murmur and rumblings of life on the ward crept back into his senses. He looked along the corridor, helpless and hopeless, but found no help there. Turning back to look to the nurses station a familiar face appeared from a side room, a face he had come to recognise over the last month.

Usually she greeted him with a happy smile and some reassuring words, letting him know that everybody was doing everything they could. Not today. He supposed that no matter how many times you had to give people bad news – the worst news – it never got easy. Her face betrayed her as she tried to be matter of fact, even though they had all known this day was coming soon, it had still caught everybody by surprise. All the nurse had to offer were platitudes, standard feel-good phrases recycled for each new relative needing comfort. He didn't mind this, he understood how hard it must be and he did feel comforted. In spite of the slightly impersonal nature of it, it was well-intentioned.

"Can I see her?"

"Of course you can love, I'm afraid she's already been taken downstairs though."

He couldn't help thinking that this was a particularly unfortunate turn of phrase in the circumstances, but didn't say so.

"We wouldn't normally move someone so quickly, but we've got an emergency coming in and needed the bed. I'm so sorry.

A short time later he stood in the corridor once more. In one hand he held a meagre bag of possessions and belongings; a watch, some unopened Jelly Babies, an unstarted crossword puzzle book. In the other some leaflets and directions for the morgue, which for obvious reasons was not widely signposted around the hospital. He read them then sat down on the nearest blue plastic chair, bolted to the floor with its companions, and sobbed as the world shuffled, rolled and walked on around him.

It was late in the evening now, time for the hospital to start settling down for the night. Although it never truly sleeps the pace changes, the light fades and the sounds become more distant, as if retreating to a safe distance to regroup and prepare to start over tomorrow.

The police woman who had tended him on the pavement earlier had been waiting for him when he was wheeled out of the ambulance. She had stayed diligently by his side until he was safely settled into a curtained off cubicle.

"I'm going off shift now Chris, I'll come back tomorrow to see about getting a statement from you if that's okay."

"That's fine, have a good night."

"You too, well, as good as you can."

"I'll try."

He didn't think he'd succeed though, his shoulder felt like it had been folded in on itself, and every movement was likely to send lances of pain through every nerve ending on the right side of his body. His palm was torn and bloody where he had fallen on it and his back hurt. He tried to lie still, which made the small of his back throb in time with his shoulder, until it reached a crescendo of pain and he had to shift slightly to get comfortable again. This adjustment reminded his shoulder that it too was supposed to be telling him something, and so the cycle perpetuated itself.

A flurry of staff had tried to make him as comfortable as they could, which wasn't very. He was now waiting for the doctor to come back with his x-rays and let him know how bad the damage was. He heard footsteps approaching his quiet space and looked up expecting to the young doctor who had seen him earlier to appear.

"Chris, what happened? Oh my god, are you okay? I mean, obviously not, but will you be?"

"Hi Bev, you really didn't need to come, you've got enough on already, I'm fine really."

"You're not, you look awful."

"Yeah, fair enough, I feel pretty awful too really. They think the collar bone's broken and I've got a few bruises, nothing major."

"Oh, is that all?"

"Sarcasm isn't your thing Bev."

"No, and gravity clearly isn't yours. What happened?"

Chris gave her a brief synopsis of the evening's chain of events, when he described what had happened to Kiera she interrupted;

"Is she okay?"

"She'll have a black eye, but she got in the cab safely. Maybe you could check up on her tomorrow, make sure she's alright."

"Of course, go on then."

Chris finished the story, ending with his present predicament. Before Bev had chance to bombard him with a further barrage of questions the doctor came back and shared the good news that the collar bone break was a nice neat one, but the orthopaedic surgeon would want to look again tomorrow and they wanted to keep an eye on him, so they were keeping him in overnight. Best of all, she was organising some pain relief for him.

Everything moved at the hospital's leisurely pace, Chris eventually ended up on a ward after midnight where he convinced Bev that it was safe to leave him for the night. She departed reluctantly, taking his house keys so she could collect some essentials for him and bring them to him the next morning. He sat propped on a mound of pillows. in a stupor of morphine induced sleeping wakefulness, as the small hours came and went.

As he dozed he was back in the street, running for his life. This time he didn't trip, instead he felt his legs straightening, he felt the bones creak and complain as they grew longer and the muscles around them grew more solid. His feet, now unimpeded, pounded the pavement. Moving faster and faster the world became a blur around him and the sound of the wind whistling past his ears became a banshee howl, drowning out the sound of his pursuer as it receded into the distance. In other moments of snatched sleep the outcome was different, his assailant catching him and inflicting a burst of exquisite agony which would wake Chris with a start as a real burst of pain made itself known.

By the time the hospital was waking, stretching its long corridors and drawing in a gulp of fresh morning air through its filtered lungs, Chris was finally in a state of deep sleep. When he woke the world was already in full flow around him. Nurses were making sure the night had not taken any unpaid dues while the world slumbered, orderlies were making sure everything was clean, in place and ready for the coming day and the patients were slowly waking and watching. As he saw an elderly man with a walking frame head off to his ablutions Chris realised he too needed to go.

Tentatively and slowly he sat himself up, using the bed rail and his good arm to pull himself forward. He gently rotated himself and slid his feet and legs over the side of the mattress and shuffled himself forward on his bottom. Every movement jarred his shoulder, which felt as though it had been filled with broken glass. It made his back hurt and he vowed to never take such a simple operation as getting out of bed for granted again. His feet finally touched down on the cool, blue vinyl floor and he started to put his weight on them.

Immediately there was a song of mocking pain. He hadn't noticed last night, maybe the other parts of him had demanded priority, or maybe he had been wheeled everywhere. He now realised that to add to his other aches, pains, worries and woes he could add a sprained ankle to his list of injuries.

He greeted this new discovery out loud,

"Ah, shit, fuck!"

The outburst finally drew the attention of a passing nurse who came to his side. Her name badge identified her as being called Grace, her broad shoulders and hips did not speak of gracefulness, but her kindly face and smile told a different story.

"Where are we off to then?"

"I need to pee."

"Well it's probably best if you hold on here, I'll pop and get you a bottle."

"I'm fine, I just need a hand to get moving."

"No, you need to stay where you are." Grace looked at the clipboard on the end of his bed.

"It says we need to check your urine for blood, so you stay here and I'll be right back."

She was as quick as she had promised to be, by the time she had whisked the curtains round his bed and passed him the bottle he was more than willing to pee into anything. He sighed with relief as the last few drops came out, then was unsure what to do with the warm plastic bottle, only that he didn't want to sit holding it on his lap. He was about to put it on the side when the curtain rustled and Grace called through:

"Knock, knock, are you done?"

"Yes, thanks."

"That's great, I'll take that away for you. Breakfast will be along soon, can you hold on or do you want a cup of tea now?"

"I'll hold on thanks."

He shuffled painfully back onto the bed while Grace adjusted his pillows and helped him back to a sitting position. He leaned back, wincing, and closed his eyes as the pain from the movement subsided.

Footsteps approached and the curtain rustled again, he hoped it was Grace with some paracetamol and a drink – he needed both. Instead he was greeted by Bev's smiling face.

"Morning, did I wake you?"

"No, I was already awake."

"How are you feeling today? You still look like shit."

"Thanks, it hurts – everywhere."

"It looks like it, can I get you anything?"

"Cup of tea? I just turned one down but I think I was a bit hasty."

"I'm on it, you stay here."

"Ha ha!"

The day passed in a series of conversations, examinations and investigations with doctors, nurses and specialists. Chris was checked, prodded, strapped up, taped together and questioned between dozing and talking with Bev who was reluctant to leave his side. Chris thought she must have better things to do, important family stuff, but was glad she stayed and offered some distractions along with a supply of sweets and mars bars from the hospital shop.

Eventually, late in the afternoon, it was decided that he could go home. Of course, that didn't mean he could go home, not until the doctor had seen him one last time, a crutch had been procured, meds had been obtained from the hospital pharmacy and Bev had collected some clothes for him as his had been cut off the night before. PC Hussain did not make an appearance that day, Chris imagined that they were dealing with the fallout from what had been a busy night, he expected she would turn up at home sometime.

The journey from hospital to home in Bev's car was tortuous, contorting himself to get in and out without moving any of the parts that hurt and suffering the lumps and bumps of what now seemed to be a horribly uneven road surface. Finally he was laying on the settee with a mound of pillows and a blanket as Bev rifled through his kitchen finding him something to eat. He closed his eyes and let home wrap it's safe, comfortable arms around him.

CHAPTER 31

AT HOME

With the aid of some strong painkillers, kindly provided by the hospital, Chris slept undisturbed on the sofa for several hours, until their effects started to wear off. PC Hussain turned up the next morning. The omnipresent Bev, (didn't she have anything better to do?) made them tea and fussed around until she was happy that they had everything they needed. Chris recounted his version of the previous evenings events while PC Hussain took copious notes, occasionally asking him supplementary questions or to pause while she caught up.

The retelling made Chris feel slightly lightheaded. The realisation of what he had done, the recklessness of it, and the knowledge that – but for blind luck – it could have ended in disaster. Not that his bloodied and broken body felt particularly triumphant, but it could have been so much worse.

The rest of the day drifted by in a fug of waking sleep, accompanied by waves of pain. Bev stayed the whole day, unknown to Chris she had assured the medical staff she would do this in order to secure Chris's swift release. She was attentive, without making too much fuss, which was good as Chris hated fuss.

Eventually the day wound down,

"I think I'm going to turn in now." He announced.

"Aren't you going to sleep down here?"

"It's okay, I can get upstairs."

"Well, I'll help if you need it."

"I'll be fine."

He wasn't fine. He had to stop more than once, Bev gently pushing him forward with her hand firmly in the small of his back to help him keep his balance as he limped and teetered up the stairs. Once there he hobbled to the bathroom, no more bottles thanks. He successfully completed this, then stood, with one hand holding his weight on the sink, and examined himself. Beneath the familiar scars and features reflected in the brightly lit mirror he could see the stubble, bags, deathly pallor and bruises of someone who truly did look like shit.

Bev was on hand to help him shuffle out of his trousers and prop him up as comfortably as she could. She bought a glass of water and his tablets and put them on his bedside table next to his phone and book.

"I've got to shoot off now, I've got some things to sort out. Call me if you need anything, otherwise I'll be back later."

"You don't need to do that Bev, I'll be fine now. Thanks for everything though."

"You'll be fine? Seriously? You couldn't even get your socks off."

"I'm sure it'll have eased up by tomorrow."

"Do you think I became deaf when the doctor told you to rest up for at least a week?" Or did you not hear her say that?"

Chris made a doomed attempt at a shrug, then winced and reconsidered as his shoulder reminded him that it was not in a moving kind of mood.

"I'll see you later."

"Okay, thanks. I'll pay you back sometime."

"Just focus on getting better and try and get some sleep. Goodnight."

"Okay, goodnight."

The door closed downstairs, leaving the house quiet and empty. In spite of the fact he felt tired Chris could not get to sleep. He shuffled and shifted trying to get into a position that was at least half tolerable. Finally, resigned to another night of seeing all the hours, he picked his book up from the bedside table. He had started it a while back but was still only a small way in, it was a slender volume that he could hold comfortably in one hand, and he read.

Predictably, now he was doing something, his eyes started to slip closed. The book fell into his lap, waking him with a start. He looked across the room to the desk, hoping Poquelin would be there. Some distraction while he couldn't sleep would be good. He was there, slumped back against the wall beside the computer. His face, not pretty at the best of times, looked even grumpier than normal. He did not greet Chris, just glared.

"How are you?"

No reply.

"I've been in the wars, please don't start throwing things around today."

Still no reply. Poquelin looked upwards and pointed his eyes away from Chris.

"I should tell you what happened really, it's the sort of story I think you'd enjoy."

More eye-rolling, followed by slump shouldered silence.

"Well, it all started when I went to the pub...."

Chris recounted the tale of the previous evenings exploits again. When he had done this earlier, he had become quite upset by the end of the retelling. PC Hussain had told him this was quite normal and it was probably the shock catching up with him. Now, freshly numbed with painkillers, he felt a touch of pride, a hint of bravado as he talked about the way he had faced up to Kiera's aggressor. He gave much less emphasis to the running away and falling over element of the story this time round.

Poquelin did not interrupt. He said nothing at all, just sat looking towards the window. Chris wondered what he was seeing out there in the darkness. He was sure those large red eyes could see in the dark, but what were they seeing now? He asked the question, but Poquelin's response was to wrap his wings around his huddled body in one surprisingly quick and graceful movement and carry on staring. Chris slipped off into restless sleep again. Next time he woke Poquelin was gone.

CHAPTER 32

NOT NOW

P olly was waiting when Bev got home, she had hardly got through the door before she was being bombarded with questions about what had happened and was she alright and was Chris okay? Polly had met Chris a few times, mostly at Potters, over the years. She liked, him, he was kind to her, funny and quiet at the same time and made you feel like he was listening to you. Mostly she liked the wicked way he would take down people he didn't have time for.

Eventually Polly was convinced that Chris's demise wasn't imminent and discussion moved on to their current 'situation' as they made supper together. She had been busy gathering whatever information she could, diving deep into the internet and making phone calls. She presented Bev with a ring binder full of notes. Inside, neatly annotated pages were filed, labelled, sorted and indexed. Everything they needed to know and do over the coming months while things got sorted out.

The actuality of it overwhelmed Bev. Chris has presented an excellent distraction for a while, but now her own predicament was back in full force.

"Here Mum, have a tissue, it's okay, we'll do this together."

"What if I don't want to do it? Any of it?"

"That's fine, everything you need is there. It's ready for you when you need it, waiting."

"Can't I just, you know, carry on?"

"What pretend nothing's happened?"

"Well, I suppose if you want to put it like that…"

"It's okay, honestly. You don't have to do anything now, but sooner or later Dad's going to be in touch, you'll need to think about it then. At least you need to sort out the money. When you're ready for all that, it's here."

She put her finger on the folder and smiled as she pushed it gently back across the table. Bev picked it up.

"I will have a look at it, but not now. Thanks love, I don't know what I'd do without you."

A kiss on the forehead and a gentle brush of Polly's hair, tucking it behind her ear, was enough to make Polly grimace and run her own hands back through her hair.

"Alright, dish up the food, I'm planning on watching Dirty Dancing again, I've already got it ready to play."

"Okay, okay, I'm on it. Do not start without me."

CHAPTER 33

KISS AND MAKE UP

Over the next few days the pain started to subside. It was always there, with an occasional shooting reminder of how bad it could be if it wanted to, if he didn't move carefully. His ankle was taking his weight again, complaining - but taking it, as he made the journey from sofa to kitchen and back. He was also getting better at doing things one-handedly, some more competently than others, thank goodness for the elasticated waist of his joggers.

Bev visited regularly and stayed for long periods, bringing round shopping, sorting out laundry and keeping him company. The days passed relatively quickly, watching TV, reading, listening to music. The nights were slower, regularly waking when he rolled onto his shoulder, seeing the clock at times that most people were deep in dreams, living out their wildest fantasies or confronting their deepest fears. Like them he dreamed in his snatches of sleep, on waking his dreams did not fade into non-memories as wakefulness and the trials of the day took over. His dreams all seemed to revolve around one short period of his life from the previous week, and that stayed with him throughout the day until they were refreshed the following night.

At night Poquelin continued to sulk sullenly on the desk, watching, saying nothing. Chris tried to engage him, tried to talk with him or rile him into speaking, but to no avail, Poquelin just sulked.

Bev was in the kitchen cooking. Chris had tried to help, resulting in some spilt rice and him being despatched to the sofa to prop himself up on his nest of cushions and pillows.

"I read your blog you know?" She called from the other room.

"Eh?"

"Your blog, I read it."

"What? My.. How did you..?"

"Mr Angree eh? You sure are."

"Yeah, well…" He had been caught unaware by this turn of events and didn't quite know how to respond, but he was glad Bev wasn't in the room to witness his embarrassment.

"Actually, I thought it was funny. You can't half rant, like one of those comedians off the telly."

"Thanks, I think. I just need to vent sometimes."

"Mind you, some of those people that write in the comments, they're angry. I think some of them really need help."

"You can say that again, some are real nut jobs."

"I wouldn't like to meet some of them in a dark alley."

"I think they're mostly like that because they're not in a dark alley, it's easy to be brave when you're safe at home."

"I expect so, even so, they can be a bit scary. I'd rather not run into them."

Chris thought of some of the hate-filled, vitriolic, bigoted comments that had been attached to some of his blogs and was keen to change the subject;

"How're things at home?"

"Come and sit in here and I'll tell you, tea's ready. Do you want me to cut it up for you?"

"For Christ's sake….yes, yes please cut it up, I'm coming."

He rolled off the settee and moved slowly and carefully to the kitchen table. Bev greeted him with a smile and a plate of food, carefully cut into bite-size pieces.

"Thanks Bev, that looks delicious. I can't tell you how much I appreciate this, everything you're doing."

"Well, if you can't help out a friend when they need it what can you do? I'm still so proud of you for rescuing Kiera like that. She's a nice kid really you know."

"I know, she works hard too. It's a shame we got off on the wrong foot."

"Well, that was hardly your fault, but yes it was a shame."

"How is she?"

"She came back to work today; she's still got one hell of a shiner. Nowhere near your standard of course, but it still looks bad."

"Poor thing. Anyway, you were going to tell me how it's going with Dave."

"Oh yeah, well the short version is he's playing nice. He's trying to sort everything out with an even split, no fuss. My solicitor says it's because he knows that I could get more if we pushed for it, but that would drag everything out for longer. I'd really rather get this over with, I feel so stupid."

"Not stupid at all, he should have been honest with you."

"I know, I'm still trying not to be angry, it must have been hard for him."

"You know what your problem is? You're too nice."

"Shut up and finish your dinner."

207

"I expect his solicitor is in touch with yours, figuring out how they can both make the most from it. They're all in it together you know."

"Yeah, maybe you should write a blog about it."

"Ha ha! Nice tea thanks."

He had just finished chasing the final remnants of his food around the plate with his fork when, with impeccable timing, the doorbell rang.

"I'll get it."

"Thanks, probably PC Hussain again."

There hadn't been many visitors over the weekend, aside from Bev. Tim had dropped by with some 'get better beers' and a promise to come back when he wasn't on his way to a paediatric appointment. PC Hussain had dropped in to check up on him and update him on what was being done. Still not much to report there, but they wanted him to make a fuller statement when he was feeling better and to ask if he would mind being a witness in court to help bolster their case. She had assured him that there would be retribution for all those involved.

Indistinct voices came from the hallway, Bev and another female voice. Then the front door closed and two pairs of footsteps came towards the kitchen.

"It's someone to see you Chris, I just need to pop up to the loo."

She turned towards the stairs, revealing a familiar looking figure standing in the doorway. Dyed blonde hair, full make up, with a long red coat over her pink sweater and leggings, all trying to deny her age. There, standing in front of him was Janet bloody Cox.

Awkwardness hung between them, she looked as uncomfortable as he felt and her eyes darted around the room, finally settling on Chris. He stared back, a whirlwind of emotions all clamouring to say the things he had been holding back for all these years. After seconds that seemed to drag out for an eternity Janet broke the silence;

"I know I'm probably the last person you want to see, but thank you. Thank you for helping my baby girl, it scares me to death thinking what might have happened if it hadn't been for you."

She proffered the small potted plant she had been holding, stepping forward and placing it on the table.

"For what it's worth, I'm sorry, so very sorry."

Chris looked at the orchid and saw the tear in Janet's eye. He put his hand on the red ceramic plant pot and felt the residue of the warmth of her hand.

"Thank you, it's beautiful. I've got just the place for it too. Do you want a cup of tea?"

"No, I don't want to bother you."

"It's no bother, I was going to put the kettle on anyway."

He grunted as he shifted his weight ready to stand up just as Bev reappeared. Chris suspected that she had never been too far away.

"Don't get up, I'll get that. Here Janet, can you grab some mugs from the cupboard please?"

Janet was surprised into action and together they made three mugs of tea. As they finished Bev produced her phone from her pocket.

"Can you excuse me for a minute? I just need to give Polly a quick call."

Janet bought the remaining mugs of tea to the table and sat opposite Chris, awkward and clearly uncomfortable. Chris asked how Kiera was doing and they managed some stilted conversation as they sipped the tea and Janet described the colour of Kiera's bruise. Chris could relate to this having seen the purples, blues and yellows of his own damaged body parts in the mirror that morning. They both agreed that the now former boyfriend should be punished to the full extent of the law.

In the background the kitchen speaker had been chuntering away to itself, largely ignored. The Love Cats by The Cure started playing, it's distinctive intro clearly audible in a moment of silence.

"Oh god, I love this song. It's one of my favourites."

"Really?" asked Chris.

"You bet, it's on just about every playlist I put together."

"Me too, good choice. What about Siouxsie?"

"Also on nearly every playlist, anything from Superstition."

"I prefer Join Hands, but Superstition is a good choice."

They ran through their favourite tracks, and some more bands that they liked in common. Chris started to realise that they were less opposite than he had always assumed.

"How come I didn't know you were into all this when we were...." Janet's voice trailed off as she mentally answered her own question and left an awkward silence.

"Anyway, I do need to be off now, again, thank you for looking after Kiera."

"No problem, you say hi to her from me. I'll be back at work soon."

"Listen, I know I was, well, you know?"

"I do know, yes. I think maybe I didn't always help myself that much either sometimes."

"No, that's not it."

"It is though, we all make mistakes – and I make my fair share. Falling into the fire for a start."

This last comment elicited a small involuntary smile from Janet as she realised it was a joke.

"Teenagers just aren't programmed to make good choices. It's lucky we grow out of it."

Janet was now crying, this was not how Chris had always imagined this meeting. He had envisioned his burning resentment leading to a bitter and angry showdown, in which he would naturally come out on top. But this? He had to admit that this was hard, being beneficent and forgiving had never been part of his imagined plan. It had changed things that they both shared a concern for somebody else's welfare, and seeing her maternal concern had changed his perception. The anger and hurt burned in the recesses of his mind, but seeing that single tear roll down her cheek he realised that this was not what he wanted at all.

Again, Bev reappeared at the most opportune of moments, she passed the tissues to Janet and put an arm around her shoulder.

"Hey, you're okay now. Are you sure you don't want another cuppa?"

"No thanks, I really do have to get going. Can I, that is, could me and Kiera pop round another day? I know she wants to say thank you, but she's a bit nervous."

"Um, yeah. Not a problem at all, it would be nice to see her. I'm here all the time at the moment."

"Good. Well, not good, but we'll see you later in the week. She really likes working at the garden centre you know?"

"Well, she's earned her place, she works hard and she's good."

They left it at that, Bev saw Janet out while Chris moved himself back to the sitting room. Bev joined him;

"Well?"

"Well, what?"

"That was nice wasn't it?"

"Yes, I suppose so, a bit of a surprise."

"You did fine; it could have been so awkward. From what I've heard you'd have been entitled to still be mad at her."

"I guess sometimes you just have to let things go. It still felt awkward though."

"Nonsense, you were the perfect gentleman."

"It seemed like the right thing, she's pretty shaken up about what happened to Kiera isn't she?"

"Who wouldn't be? Thank goodness you were there in your cape and tights."

"Leave it out, you're making me blush. How about a cup of tea?"

"You've got it – even though you didn't say please."

CHAPTER 34

IDIOT

That night Poquelin broke his silence;
"I'm so disappointed in you."

Chris had just settled down, expecting another quiet night while Poquelin sat moodily on the desk. Now he was standing beside the bed, his eyes at the same level as Chris's as he lay in his carefully arranged pile of pillows. He turned his head slightly to look at him.

"What?"

"You could've really let rip, you had her here, at your mercy."

"Why would I do that? What good would that have done?"

"I can't believe you're asking that. What good? After making your life hell, after prize day? Payback, that's what good it would have done."

"But it wouldn't have made anything better would it?"

"It would have evened the scoreboard a bit, you had her stone cold. You could have had her in tears in minutes."

"She was in tears anyway, poor woman."

"Aagh! Look at you, all busted up and not even able to wipe your own arse. It's all her kid's fault, and you're worried about her. You should've gone to town on her."

"No I shouldn't, it would've been wrong."

"But...."

"No! It would've been wrong. I may look like a monster but I don't have to act like one. Some good may come of this."

"It won't, she'll forget, they all will. Who's ever been nice to you?"

Chris had an epiphany; it suddenly occurred to him that people were nice to him. Not just the doctors and nurses who were paid to be, but others. Bev for starters, Tim and Deb, Roger, in fact he had a large number of people who he knew, but kept at arm's length so they didn't have the chance to hurt him. Maybe now was the time to change things, maybe now was the time to reinvent himself and start to make the most of the people he had.

"I've got friends."

Poquelin looked at him. Chris didn't know if he was reading his thoughts or just guessing, but his expression changed. For the first time he saw Poquelin's face show something resembling regret mixed with confusion.

"I was wrong about you; I thought we were on the same side. I thought we were friends."

"Why the fuck would you think that? You've never done anything but torment me."

"Wrong. I've tried to offer you guidance and motivation. I've tried to help you see the way things really are. I've tried to help you."

"Well, with friends like you I don't need enemies, do I? Why don't you piss off and bother someone else?"

Poquelin glowered, his body trembled and quivered slightly and Chris braced himself for the coming explosion. He fancied he could feel the temperature rising in the room and could hear the distant sound of screaming and faintly smell an acrid burning odour.

"You are no fun anymore." Poquelin slumped, his wings fell to his side and he turned away. Chris exhaled the breath he hadn't realised he'd been holding and closed his eyes.

The grating scrape of the window made him fully alert again, what now? He rolled out of bed and took the two steps to get him to the window, his shoulder singing at the unexpected movement. He put his good hand on the window frame to pull it closed and looked out into the darkness.

Under the streetlight he saw a small black figure with its back to him. Over one shoulder it held a stick with a bulging bundle wrapped in black cloth tied to the end, like a macabre Dick Whittington. Over the other shoulder Poquelin raised his hand, without looking backwards or slowing his pace he popped up his clawed middle finger and kept it raised as he passed through the pool of light and disappeared into the shadows beyond. Chris stayed watching for a moment or two, then shivered. He pulled the window shut and repositioned himself in the bed, where he slept soundly.

CHAPTER 35

NEW HORIZONS

Bev's visits became less frequent as Chris's body healed and he was able to do more for himself. When she arrived with bags of food and newspapers they mostly sat and drank tea as she provided details of the comings and goings of the world outside. She made adjustments to the garden under Chris's guidance, moving pots into the nurturing warmth of the house where they would spend the winter, deadheading flowers and planting some bulbs she bought him from work. Mostly she just kept him company as they both licked their wounds and slowly prepared for whatever it was that would come next.

Tim made a return visit, this time Deb accompanied him. Together they showed off a new and updated black and white picture of what appeared to be another small ghost, but was, they assured him, their baby. To be fair, Chris could make out more of its features this time. They were on their way back from the scan and he was the first person they had been able to show it off to. Conversation ranged from the baby, a rehash of the events at the Crown, and Chris's recuperation. Deb went up to the loo and Chris asked about the new job;

"It's okay, the guys are alright, but it's so corporate. Everything is by the book; they don't want ideas. It's not a problem, I just go in and get things done, but it feels so…I don't know…unfriendly. It's just not as nice as Potters."

"Maybe you're still getting to know people."

216

"No, it isn't that, everybody's on different shift patterns and rotas. It feels like I never seem to work with the same person twice."

"You just need to give it time then."

"I don't know, it doesn't seem to be getting better. They don't ask me anything that's not my job either, like when we used to plan orders together. Now it's just 'there's the order, unload it'."

Deb came back from the bathroom;

"Are you moaning about work again? Why don't you just ask if you can go back to Potters now Lagrange is going? Who's replacing him, do you know yet?"

"No, not yet. Although I've been a bit out of the loop recently."

"I suppose so, Bev not said anything?"

"I don't think she knows anything either, she hasn't mentioned it."

"How's she doing?" asked Deb.

"Yeah, okay considering. She'll be sorry she missed you two, she usually pops over in the morning but she had to go to the solicitors this morning."

"Poor thing, I need to give her a call and arrange to go out for a coffee or something. I bet she's not getting much girl talk here."

"You're probably right, she'd like that. I'll warn her when she comes round."

By the time they left Chris felt drained, he was surprised at how even small interactions were still leaving him feeling tired, absolutely zonked. He flopped carefully back on the settee, pulled a blanket over himself and fell asleep.

The ring of the doorbell pulled him back from the depths of his sleep. It felt as if he had only just closed his eyes, but a glance at the clock as he untangled himself from the blanket told a different story.

"Hang on, I'm coming."

He didn't hurry, assuming it was Bev on her way back from her appointment without his spare key.

"I'm on my way."

Nearly at the door now,

"Okay, okay, I'm here."

He opened the door to a familiar looking man in a suit and a big smile, although Chris could not immediately place where he knew him from. He smiled back and waited for the man to speak, hoping it would jog his memory and give some clue as to who this mystery caller was.

"Hi Chris, I don't know if you remember me…"

As soon as he heard the gentle Welsh accent it came back to him. He was from head office, his name still eluded Chris, Lagrange had briefly introduced him last year when he had visited Potters.

"…my name is…"

Now it came back to him, the highly implausible;

"James Dean, yes I remember. Uh, come in. Sorry it's a bit of a muddle at the moment. How can I help?"

"Thanks, and no need to apologise, I understand how difficult it must be right now."

He stepped inside and Chris guided him past the front room with its dishevelled settee into the kitchen where, thankfully, Deb had tidied and washed up before she left. He invited his visitor to sit down while he started to boil the kettle.

"Would you like tea or coffee?"

"Coffee would be great if it's no bother, can I help?"

"It's okay thanks, I've got it. Milk and sugar?"

"Neither, just black thanks."

"Have you driven over from Cardiff?"

"Yes, I had a meeting with Gavin about his new job. He told me about your act of bravery, how you stepped up to help another GardenCo employee. I hope you don't mind me popping over and seeing how you're doing?"

Great, thought Chris, now his moment of foolhardy recklessness had been elevated to 'an act of bravery'.

"No, that's fine. I'm mending up now thanks."

"Well, don't rush things. I'm letting you know that, given the circumstances, you can take as long as you need without HR harassing you. From the sounds of it you may have saved that young lady's life. Nice coffee, thanks."

"You're welcome, and thank you too."

"No problem. Now, I don't want to talk shop while you're recovering but Gavin tells me that you know more about the garden centre here than anybody, including him."

'Especially him', thought Chris.

"I'm sure he's exaggerating."

"I'm pretty sure he's not, you've been there longer than anyone haven't you?"

Chris supposed this was true since old Sid had retired last year,

"I suppose I have now, yes."

"Well then, is it okay if I pick your brains for a few minutes?"

"No, that's fine."

Three cups of tea, two coffees and half a packet of biscuits later Chris's brain felt as if it had been picked clean. He'd been careful not to badmouth Lagrange, but didn't hold back on his opinions about how the centre had been turned into a glorified gift shop. He had given this a great deal of thought over time, and had plenty of information to help make his point thanks to the time he spent looking at invoices, orders and spreadsheets.

"You see somebody coming in to buy a present for someone and they might spend 20 or 30 pounds. Now, a serious gardener will spend more than that on one plant, if it's something unusual or special. But gardeners are passionate, they rarely buy just one plant. There are local growers who can produce those kinds of plants, in fact they would enjoy the challenge of it. There's not much mark-up in pansies and geraniums and the big suppliers undercut them all the time. I've spoken to some of the growers and we reckon it's doable."

"So can you do it then?"

"In theory, yes."

"No, I mean can *you* do it?"

"Eh?"

"Could you do that, get the growers to sign up and get the serious gardeners coming in. Make it a place that people will travel for miles to visit?"

"I just do the books really."

"Well, here's the thing, Gavin thought you might be the ideal person to take over from him."

"But, eh? What?"

Chris couldn't find the words to ask if this was some elaborate wind up. He couldn't articulate a coherent response to something that hadn't even been phrased as a question in the first place.

"I don't need an answer right now, you need to focus on getting better. But it's a serious offer, I hope you'll consider it."

"So this was an interview then?"

"Kind of, I like your ideas, hopefully we can use it as a model for other centres."

"Well, can I let you know?"

"Of course, I need to get going now, it's a long drive back. I'll come back next week, I'll give you some warning next time, and we'll talk again. Now, if I could just use your bathroom please, then I'll let myself out and you can get on with your day."

Chris sat in the house, alone and silent. He was confused about what had just happened, unsure if this turn of events was a golden opportunity or a poison chalice. He picked up his phone and called Bev.

CHAPTER 36

DESIRABLE OUTCOMES

"*H*i, Bev speaking, can I help you?"

A pause as she listened.

"No, I'm sorry he's not in the office right now. Can I put you on hold for a moment?"

Several clicks and presses of the phone.

"Hi Tim, is he there with you? …Oh good, I thought he might be, you're not showing him baby photos by any chance are you?"…Ha, I knew it. I'm putting a call through to him, it's Joe from Hill Farm…Ok, thanks Tim, can you remind him I'm leaving early too please?...Okay, thanks, putting the call through now."

Some more buttons were pressed, then Bev put down her own phone. She picked up a small pile of papers that needed signing and took them across the office and placed them on the other desk. She looked up at the painting over the desk, horses outside a barn or stable. Chris assured her it was valuable, the picture framer had told him somewhere in the four digit range. She didn't mind it, but wouldn't want it in her sitting room particularly. She guessed maybe Chris didn't either, otherwise it wouldn't be here, would it? She gathered up her coat and bag and went out to reception.

"Hi Kiera, I'm off now. Chris is down with Tim, give him a shout if you need anything."

"Okay, it's pretty quiet now, I think I've got it all under control."

"Alright, have a good afternoon, see you tomorrow."

"You too, hope it all goes okay."

"Thanks, bye."

She drove the short distance to a small row of terraced houses where she parked and got out. Polly was already there, waiting. Bev checked her watch as she walked towards her.

"I'm not late am I?"

"No, I'm early, I couldn't wait."

"Okay, phew. He should be here any moment."

As she spoke another car pulled into a free space and a young man in a blue suit got out. He leant back into the car collected some things from the passenger seat then turned and walked towards them smiling. He held up his right hand and shook a bunch of keys that jangled and sparkled as they reflected the afternoon sunlight.

"This is my favourite bit. Who wants them?"

Polly held her hand out and took the keys from him as Bev was proffered the clipboards and shown where to sign the several duplicate forms attached to it. Transaction completed they thanked the man who was still only half way back to his car by the time Polly had opened the front door of number 17.

"It's ours?"

"All ours, a fresh start. Somewhere for you to stay for however long you want when you and Fred get back from New Zealand."

"Love you mum."

A hug and a kiss.

"I'm sure your dad would still love to see you too sometimes."

"Yeah, well, we'll see. I'm not sure I'm quite ready for that yet."

"When you are though, give him a chance. I know he wants to see you."

"You're too nice you are."

They both looked around the bare hallway and through the door to the empty kitchen. Everything was waiting to be bought to life and turned into a home.

*

Chris walked back into reception, pausing to adjust some succulents on the way, getting them to show their best sides to passers-by.

"Bev said to remind you she was leaving early, she went about 10 minutes ago."

"Okay, thanks Kiera. Everything okay here?"

"Yes, a few calls asking when the Oxalis are coming in, people can't wait."

"I think they're coming on Thursday, you can check with Tim."

"That's good, I told them by the end of the week."

"Well, I hope I ordered enough now, we'll see. Changing the subject, how's mum?"

"She's fine, she said to tell you that she liked the Pixies album."

"Good, I thought she would."

"It all sounds dreadful to me, old music."

"Rude, it's better than some of the stuff the radio bombard you with."

"So you say."

They both laughed at this and Chris went into the office.

The door swung open and Chris stepped inside, pushing it firmly shut behind him. For a moment he just stood, listening, thinking, pausing. Then he smiled to himself, he looked up at the painting of the horses - so much better here than dominating the sitting room. Having crossed the room he took the pile of waiting papers from the tray and settled down at his desk.

Steve Beed was born in 1964, since then he has seen men walking on the moon, been chased by a wild elephant and been on the TV – which makes it sound all much more exciting than it actually was. He has a beautiful wife and three grown up children and has been a teacher since finishing college in 1987.

You can write and tell me how much you liked this book at:
stevebeed64@gmail.com
I will let you know about new books that are in the offing.

You can follow my blog at:

https://steevbeed.wordpress.com

Printed in Great Britain
by Amazon

32553087R00126